Diving into the tunnel, I pounded through the corrugated tube until I reached a mobile home park on the other side. The first two houses were dark, and I was afraid it would take too long to wake anyone up. At the third house, where the lights were on, I sped up the four steps and frantically banged on the door. A wide-eyed, elderly woman peered at me through the glass. "Please, help me," I gasped. "You don't have to let me in. Just call the police. Someone's trying to kill me."

DANGER!
CROSS CURRENTS

AN ALIX NICHOLSON MYSTERY

DANGER!
CROSS CURRENTS

SHARON GILLIGAN

Hooray for feminist bookstores.

Sharon Gilligan

**RISING
TIDE
PRESS**

Huntington, New York

Rising Tide Press
5 Kivy Street
Huntington Station, NY 11746
(516) 427-1289

Printed in the United States on acid-free paper

Publisher's note:
All characters, places and situations in this book are fictitious and any
resemblance to persons (living or dead) is purely coincidental.

Publisher's Acknowledgments:
The publisher is grateful for all the support and expertise offered by the
members of its editorial board: Bobbi Bauer, Adriane Balaban, Beth Heyn,
Harriet Edwards and Pat G. And a special thanks to Harriet and Adriane
for their excellent proofing and criticism, to Edna G. for believing in us, and
to the feminist bookstores for being there.

First printing August 1994
10 9 8 7 6 5 4 3 2 1

Edited by Alice Frier and Lee Boojamra
Book cover art: Evelyn Rysdyk

Two line excerpt from "A Hard Death" by May Sarton is reprinted from *A
GRAIN OF MUSTARD SEED : New Poems,* with the permission of W.W.
Norton & Company, Inc. Copyright © 1971 by May Sarton.

Library of Congress Cataloging-in-Publication Data
Sharon Gilligan 1943—
          Danger! Cross Currents/ Sharon Gilligan
                    p.cm
ISBN 1-883061-01-6   93-087609

Acknowledgments

This author must once again thank the women of Rising Tide Press who continue to support and encourage my work, who enhance my words with the finest production designs one could hope for, and who are just about the best women in the world to work for.

Loving gratitude to Meadow, who reviewed the chapter alluding to women's spirituality and who gently helped to make it ring true.

Thanks must also go to the Friends of the Fort Bragg Library, who have kept the doors open in spite of severe budget cuts, and who have sponsored innovative programs such as the workshop for mystery writers with Sgt. Robert Petrey of the Mendocino County Sheriff's Department. My thanks to him as well.

And special thanks to the readers of Alix Nicholson's first adventure for wanting her to go on taking pictures and looking for the truth.

Author's Note

The characters and private institutions listed here are fictitious and bear no resemblance to any living persons or active institutions. The city of Fort Bragg and Mendocino County are real places, facing some of the real development and economic growth challenges touched upon in this book, but the officials portrayed as employees of the county are not based on any actual people working there.

Dedication

To the beautiful and strong women of the North Coast women's community who are making it feel like home: Meadow, Laurel, Lynn, Donna, Sky, Jynx, Barb, Sarah, Claire, Max, Joan, Pam, Helen, Pic, and the precious Flame, to list only a few.

And to Roberta, who dreamed we could escape the rat race and made it come true.

Prologue

I punched the eject button on the car's tape deck, interrupting the fifth go-round of Kenny Rogers and Dottie West lamenting, then postponing, their breakup for one more night. I'd heard it every sixty miles or so since leaving Dubuque, and it was time to stop feeling sorry for myself. It was the day after Labor Day, and the wide grey expanse of Interstate 90 was all mine, except perhaps for a lurking highway patrol car or two. So what if I was alone in the middle of Southern Minnesota and Gina Laurenzi was back home in Dubuque getting on with her life...without me? Actually Gina was never the great love of my life, despite the attempts of our mutual friends to link us up as a couple.

"Mutt and Jeff" or "Pepper and Salt" were among the forced, cutesy nicknames friends often used to describe us. One referred to Gina's petite frame, which I towered over at five feet ten inches, while the other contrasted her warm, dark features to my fair skin, ice blue eyes and blonde hair. But nothing they did could make us a couple or make Gina "my better half." She was just the woman I'd been sleeping with for the last year, and she had been absolutely right when she dumped me two weeks ago.

All summer we had talked about making this trip out West together. I had been invited to be the artist-in-residence for the fall term at Pacific Arts, a four-year college in Northern California, and we figured the trip might be a way to decide if we had a future. But I think we both knew we didn't.

In mid-August I had left Dubuque for a week-long seminar in Chicago on techniques for night photography, and had come home to find a curt message on my phone machine. "Alix. Gina. We need to talk. Call me."

So I went to her apartment, and after an hour of desperately hot sex, we talked. Sex is the only thing I could call it. It had little to do with making love. Mostly Gina said good-bye. Mostly I said I understood. She wanted more than a weekly sleep-over date, and I couldn't promise to be any different, any more giving of myself.

I had to admit, Gina was a warm, responsive woman and deserved a lover who really cared. But I was not ready to make a commitment. Gina had said, "We're both over forty, Alix, and maybe that doesn't bother you. But it does me. I'm too old to waste time on a relationship that's going nowhere."

In my own brittle way I had tried to make a joke of it. "What's the matter, Gina? Hearing your biological clock ticking? I'm sorry, Honey, but if you're trying to start a family, I'd be a lousy sperm donor, anyway." That's when she threw me out, calling me "the Nordic ice maiden."

I yanked the tape out of the player and flung it into the chaos that covered the floor in the back of my aging VW van. I genuinely liked Gina and even missed her a little, but in some ways, it was a relief not to have to try and meet someone else's expectations. *Yeah, right, Nicholson. If it's such a relief, then why do you feel so awful about the way it ended?* Maybe I felt bad because it was one more episode in a long string of failed relationships. At this point in my life it seemed my most enduring relationship was with my collection of cameras: some high-tech, with everything but whistles and drum rolls; others nearly antique, with burnished-wood lens boards and brass hinges.

The second passion in my life was this all-purpose van, my surrogate home. I had ripped out the back seat to make room for all the gear I lugged around, and if I piled things up just right, I could even stretch out in my sleeping bag for a nap.

I dug around the pile of music cassettes on the passenger seat looking for something upbeat. I popped in Deidre McCalla's "With a Little Luck" and gave the old yellow bus more gas, glad that I didn't have to report to my new, temporary job until September 20th. I thought about what my first long-term assignment in more than ten years would be like. As the music was trying to tell me, I *was* lucky to get an invitation to teach a full semester at this school on the North Coast of California. What else could I call it but luck when I had never had a show of my photography west of the Rockies (or east of the Alleghenies, for that matter)? Even the five volumes of my documentary work had managed only very limited distribution.

When I questioned the dean of the fine arts department, Roald Huberman, about where he'd heard of me, he had said simply that he'd been shown my work by an acquaintance and was impressed. I wanted to question him further, but I was afraid I'd sound as if I wasn't confident in the extent that my work had circulated. Would I be interested in a four-month stint teaching a class they were calling "One Picture, One Thousand Words—The Scope of Documentary Photography"?

I wasn't sure I'd ever remember the title, but the idea of working with a college class in my own field was appealing after years as a substitute, baby-sitting unruly high-schoolers or trying to follow someone else's lesson plan. "Subbing" in the Dubuque high school system was an easy way to increase my income without taking too much energy away from my photography, but it offered little intellectual stimulation.

I wondered about Huberman, who would be my immediate superior in the art department. The only Roald I had ever heard of was Roald Dahl, the author of *Charlie and the Chocolate Factory*. But Huberman's formal demeanor and clipped accent on the phone made me doubt he could be counted on for anything as whimsical as a child's fantasy. In any event, I could use this job as an excuse to stay in California through the holidays and save myself the annual tense visit with my father and stepmother. I'd manage to get along with Huberman, I was sure. After all, he had shown the good taste to like my work.

All in all, this trip and the job were a welcome change. I didn't need a lover to share my good fortune. Besides, being with Gina had never been very different from being lonely. She had said that was my fault, and she was probably right. Her exact words had been, "I don't know how you do it, Alix, but you're the first dyke I've known who makes love at arm's length. I can't seem to get close to you, and I'm tired of trying."

I was doing it again, feeling sorry for poor old Alix. Out of the corner of my eye I perceived the rich amber wheat fields of Minnesota sliding by as I pumped up the volume on Deidre. I tried to sing along. Maybe my luck would include a short, but very passionate, no-strings-attached affair. I was ready for one. I made a mental note that once I knew Huberman a little, I'd have to ask him who had shown him my work. If I had an admirer living near the Pacific Ocean, I ought to know about it.

"That woman! Someday I will get even with her!" he shouted, slamming the door behind him.

I had been standing in Roald Huberman's office, waiting for him, and now I turned abruptly at his bellow. "I beg your pardon?"

A man I guessed was Huberman blushed deeply and adjusted his wire-rimmed glasses. His voice dripping with excessive contrition, he said, "I am so sorry. You must be Ms. Nicholson. I apologize for my outburst. Please pay no attention. The faculty and staff have just had a rather, shall we say, boisterous faculty meeting." Picking up a thin manila envelope, he added, changing the subject, "This packet of information should acquaint you with our program and the campus. Please feel free to look it over at your convenience."

Recalling my goal of finding out who introduced my work to Huberman, I decided he didn't look like a man easily coaxed, and I was still reluctant to reveal any lack of confidence in my work. I studied him closely. His thickset body, made thicker by rumpled brown corduroy slacks and a bulky tan sweater, was inches shorter than mine. Pale skin, now mottled with red from embarrassment, hung loosely from his face, but it didn't seem to be the jowliness of age, rather just flaccid muscle tone. In fact, his fine-textured sandy hair and the snap in his blue-grey eyes made me think he was probably younger than I.

To get the meeting back on track quickly, I offered him my portfolio of 11 x 14 enlargements, which I had brought cross country. If he was disappointed in their quality after only seeing the small prints in books, he didn't let on.

When he looked up at me, his smile tightened the fleshy jowls, and his countenance brightened considerably. "Excellent, Ms. Nicholson. Even better in this format than your published work. I must congratulate myself for taking a chance and inviting you out here. Our students should learn a great deal from you."

Never a good recipient of praise, I nodded in his direction and mumbled a word of thanks. I loved capturing images: places, objects, people. It didn't much matter. But once they were in my camera, getting them on paper was still a struggle. Even now, more than two years after my darkroom assistant's death from AIDS-related pneumonia, I didn't feel adept at an enlarger. But after having Brian Bellamy print my work for almost eight years and seeing how his genius influenced it, I didn't trust anyone else with my negatives.

Shaking myself out of my reverie, I said, "Please, call me Alix. I know classes don't start until Monday, but when can I see my classroom and the lab?"

Huberman opened his arms expansively. "Let me show you our facilities. After the tour, I shall arrange to get you a set of keys."

"I'd like that. It will give me some time to get acquainted with the setup."

We left his sparse office and walked down a wide, well-lighted corridor lined with student work, mostly watercolor and acrylic paintings. At the end of the hall, we exited the building and followed a gravel path to a smaller, grey, cedar-sided structure about two hundred yards from the administration building. It looked like it had been built from a prefabricated kit for rapid construction. As we walked he went on, in a voice that I could only describe as a supercilious drone, to repeat what he had told me on the phone several times since our first contact last spring. My primary assignment would be an advanced class of photography students, but I would also have a beginning class and be responsible for helping them produce photographs for the spring catalog. Also, the college wanted me to organize a show highlighting the work from all the art classes, which would be exhibited in the campus art gallery.

As we walked, I reviewed what I knew of Pacific Arts. The college was set on a flat, grassy headland north of the town of Fort Bragg, on land once owned by one of the lumber companies that had built up the area. To the south, in the center of town, a towering plume of steam from the Georgia-Pacific mill confirmed that this was still timber country. The ocean was less than a quarter of a mile away from the last college building, and next to the college, a wide stream called

Pudding Creek moved slowly toward the ocean, portions of its surface covered by a dense, velvety muck.

"Here we are. I think you'll like our laboratory. While it is not state-of-the-art, it is more than adequate for your beginning class, which will meet in the evening, as well as for the morning advanced group." His voice dripped with pride at his department's resources.

The classroom had eight or ten long, sturdy folding tables, twenty or so chairs with castors, a massive light table for reviewing negatives and a variety of photo trimmers, mat cutters and a dry mount heat press that resembled an old-fashioned pants-pressing machine.

I noted with pleasure that the darkroom *was* well-equipped: twenty identical photographic enlargers, each at a spacious work station with light-tight drawers for photographic paper storage, and cabinets below for supplies. In the center of the room, a deep stainless-steel sink provided plenty of space for developing trays and print washing tanks.

"This is our black-and-white darkroom. Next door is the color darkroom." We left the room and passed through the narrow foyer that served as a light lock between the darkrooms' doors and normal room illumination. The second room was equally well-appointed with half a dozen enlargers with color heads mounted on them. Huberman was pleased at the nod of approval I gave him.

On the path back to the administration building, he asked, "Have you found a place to reside during your stay here?"

"No," I admitted. "I'm booked at the Best Western across the road for the present. I thought I'd look for something this weekend before classes start."

Huberman shook his head sagely. He seemed to have an opinion on everything. "You will find a rental difficult to procure around here, especially since you are not planning on a long-term stay. I know someone who may be able to help you—Meredith Coates. She is a member of the faculty, in the business department, and there is a cabin on her property that is currently unoccupied. It's quite reasonable, if you can stand the company. I asked her to stop by my office after her class. I hope you don't think of me as a meddler. It's just that I know the housing situation here is extremely bleak." Quickly he added, "Of course, the cabin is small so I'm sure Meredith would understand if you chose to look around a bit more."

Huberman finally stopped yammering long enough to open the door to his office, then stepped aside to let me go in first. I couldn't decide if he was meddling or if I should be annoyed, so I just shrugged.

"No harm in meeting her. I actually don't need a lot of space since I'll have the use of this darkroom facility." Then, feeling slightly uncomfortable about this residential "fix-up," I accidentally blurted out exactly what I was thinking. "Anyway, I'm a big girl, and I can say no if I don't think it's right for me."

"I hope you won't say no, even if you are a *big girl*." I turned my head toward the unfamiliar female voice, and I watched as her eyes, which were bluer than I imagined eyes could be, scanned the full length of my body until they met my gaze. Meredith Coates, I assumed, was sitting behind Huberman's desk as if she belonged there. She looked to be about my age or older, but her face was lined and leathery in a sun-worshipper way. She had a square jaw and reddish-blonde hair. The white sleeveless top she wore showed off her tanned, firm upper arms. My first reaction was, *if this was a man, she'd be Kirk Douglas in his prime.* There was even a hint of the famous cleft in the center of her chin.

"Hi, Rollie. That was quite a powwow we just had, wasn't it? I hope there aren't any hard feelings."

"Of course not, Meredith. Ultimately the best *man* will win." With a smirk that matched his superior tone, Huberman turned away from his colleague and toward me. "Ms. Nicholson, Alix, this is Meredith Coates. She teaches real estate law and zoning regulations. Meredith, Alix Nicholson, our *artist*-in-residence for the fall term." His emphasis on the word artist made me curious.

Somewhat puzzled, I said, "Real estate, zoning regs? I thought Pacific offered only a fine arts curriculum, Dr. Coates?"

Meredith stood up, swept around Huberman's desk and passed him to stand in front of me. Shorter than me by nearly six inches, she looked into my eyes with a conspiratorial grin, and said, "Why, Ms. Nicholson, haven't you ever heard of the 'Art of the Deal'? A signed contract can be a thing of beauty indeed."

Despite the smile, there was a bite in her tone I suspected was for Huberman's discomfort. With her eyes, she invited me to play along, but after driving cross country for a job, I wasn't about to blow it the first day.

I smiled back. "But how many galleries cater to collectors of mortgages?"

Her laugh was a low and hearty chuckle. "Touché, Alix, if I may call you that. And you can drop that Doctor and Professor stuff with me. I got my education the old-fashioned way, I earned it behind a desk out in the real world." She turned her back on Huberman, pointedly avoiding the glare he was aiming at her.

"Of course, Meredith. Besides, Dr. Huberman tells me you have a cottage that's available to rent, so we might end up being neighbors. When may I see it?"

Meredith looked from Huberman, then back to me. "Actually it's more like a cabin. If you're done with Rollie here, I can give you a lift out there right now. I've got to be back for a four o'clock class so we don't both need to drive."

The grunt from Huberman told me he didn't appreciate Meredith's nickname for him. Clearly, she enjoyed vexing him. I was curious about what she had done to him at the staff meeting to prompt his explosion, and wondered if I wanted to be caught between my department head and my possible landlady. After a moment's hesitation, I shrugged. "Sure. Why don't I meet you in the parking lot? There are a couple of things I'd like to pick up at my car. It's the bright yellow and black VW camper. You can't miss it."

As Meredith left, Huberman's narrowed, angry eyes followed her. I didn't know the man very well, but I needed to know what I had just stepped into the middle of.

"I'd guess you don't like her very much, Dr. Huberman. If there's a reason I might not want to rent from her, I'd sure like to know it."

"No, no, it's nothing like that." Huberman waved his hand as if shooing a gnat. "Meredith is usually civil, even cordial at times. She has opened her home to faculty gatherings and such, but, well...frankly, she's trying to take over Pacific Arts. And she has a lot of help in that with our new president, Mr. Sutter." His petulant, ominous whisper seemed laughable, but he was deadly serious.

"Take over?" was the only response I could think of.

"Well," he admitted, "I suppose not literally. But Sutter, who obtained his title only because he was related to the founder, is merely a crass money-grubber. Why, the man has never even earned a master's degree. Right now the business classes are part of a pilot program, but if they become a permanent fixture here someday, a degree from Pacific Arts College will no longer mean that the holder is an artist recognized by his or her peers as talented and committed to the pursuit of beauty. Someday, it will just be another trophy for overly indulged rich brats who couldn't tell a Monet from a Modigliani." His voice rose with his last sentence and the soft lines of his face were reddened with anger. He must have caught my look of surprise because he dropped his eyes for just a moment, then met my gaze steadily with a resigned smile.

"I am sorry. You *do* seem to have seen me at my worst today. I get a little overwrought about Pacific Arts because I'm afraid if its reputation as an arts college is destroyed, ultimately the college will disappear. I think of our founder, Sonya Abbott, turning in her grave as her greedy half-brother kills this place." With a cynical smile, Huberman added, "I guess we can surmise that artistic genius did not spring from the parent they shared."

He must have noticed my uncomfortable shifting of weight and slowly edging toward the door because he shook his head, mocking himself. "But perhaps you don't want to get embroiled in the political machinations of the academic staff, certainly not on your first day in Fort Bragg. After all, you *will* be leaving us all to our wrangling by the first of the year."

It was true that my position was only temporary, but if I was going to work in Huberman's department and, possibly, live close to Meredith Coates, I wanted a little more information to avoid potential land mines. I decided to come right out and ask, "Is it just the reputation of Pacific Arts you're worried about, or is there something else going on?"

Huberman tilted his head slightly as if an idea had just occurred to him. "Actually the reputation is vital, because there are interests in this county, including Mark Sutter, who would rather see ocean-access condos on this property. If enrollment drops and the administrative board can't meet the budget, the land-grabbing sharks will smell blood in the water. I don't know if the board would be able to hold out indefinitely if offers for this land skyrocketed."

"Isn't there anything you or the other members of the art department can do to keep it going?"

"I don't know, but as an artist yourself, I'm sure you understand our position and would want to help us preserve an institution like ours."

"Well, Dr. Huberman, I'll certainly do all I can to enhance the image of the school with the products from our documentary and beginning classes, but I don't know how else I could help."

Leaning toward me with a conspiratorial glint in his eye, his voice hissed at me softly. "Actually, there may be something you could do. If you *were* living near Ms. Coates, you might be able to provide some valuable information on the people I believe she's lining up to pounce on this property."

I'd had enough of this conversation. My first reaction was to pack up my portfolio, tell Dr. Huberman where he could stick his job and turn the VW back toward the Midwest. But I had invested a lot of time and money to travel 2,000 miles for a change in my life, and I wasn't going to let some petty academic drive me away before I'd ever stepped in front of the class.

I knew very little about Pacific's reputation, but I had been impressed that it included photography in the fine arts. That had been my crusade for years. To most people, taking pictures was just a technical skill, not an art form. I'd stopped counting the number of people who admired my work by saying, "Wow, you must have a really good camera."

I got up and collected my work from Huberman's desk. "Thank you for your comments on my work. I'll let you know where I'm staying on Monday when I pick up my class lists. I'd better not keep Ms. Coates waiting any longer." I started to leave, then turned back to make my last point very clear. "But if I do decide on renting her cabin, I intend to respect her privacy, just as I expect her to respect mine. You and I may share an appreciation for art, Dr. Huberman, but I will not betray anyone's trust."

Although the color on his cheeks turned a bright pink, he merely nodded absently as he turned his attention to some other work on his desk. It was as if he had never asked me to spy on a fellow faculty member for him. "H-hhmm. That will be fine. Enjoy your weekend, and I hope you manage to get settled somewhere. Meredith's cabin isn't so bad, if, as I said, you don't mind the company."

As I left, I realized I wasn't any closer to getting up the nerve to ask Huberman where he had seen enough of my work to offer me this residency, and now I had probably alienated him by refusing to be his informant. But it was very clear to me that finding the answer to that question was the only intrigue I wanted to be involved in this school term.

Meredith pointed her sturdy, silver, four-wheel drive Ford Explorer north. Along Highway 1 I caught glimpses of blue water, rolling surf and a rugged coastline west of the weathered barns and motels. As strangers introduced only moments earlier, Meredith and I had little to say, despite the fact that her coy remark about hoping I wouldn't say no to her cabin had prompted a knowing look between us. Perhaps it was my imagination, but neither one of us did much to conceal our "butch-ness."

In an attempt to break the ice, I commented, "Nice car."

"Thanks," she nodded. "It's a little 'dykey' for my tastes, but some of the properties I show are off of crappy, unpaved roads, narrow dirt lanes, you name it."

"And people want to develop these places?"

"Some clients are developers, others are just city people looking for someplace to escape to."

Beyond the line of motels hugging the coast, a stretch of industrial facilities lined the ocean side of the road, and, groping for conversation, I said, "It seems a shame to spoil access to this view with old tires and concrete pouring trucks."

Meredith shook her head. Through tightly clenched teeth, she spit out her sentences scornfully. "Damn shame. That kind of property is worth millions in the right hands. A good developer with some clout in Sacramento could really cash in. The road behind those businesses is what they call the haul road. Timber used to be trucked to the mill across that road. Still belongs to the lumber company. The land west of it is part of the state park system. Now some damn environmental group is buying up the road to turn *it* over to the state. What a waste!"

Almost timidly, I offered my views. "Waste? But if it becomes part of the park system, then more people can enjoy it."

"Yeah, for free." Her tone was contemptuous. I began to wonder if I'd like living so close to someone who cared about land and landscapes based solely on their monetary value. Grudgingly, Meredith pointed out the entrance to MacKerricher State Park as we passed it. "There are some interesting shots from out there. Sea scapes, nature stuff. Plus some trails and boardwalks if you like jogging or hiking."

"Sounds nice," I said, noncommittally. To change the subject, I asked, "Dr. Huberman mentioned the founder of the college, Sonya Abbott. Do you know anything about her?"

"She was a sculptor. Hear she was quite good. Originally, the grounds of the college held her private studio. Other artsy types wanted a piece of the action, and ultimately, the current buildings were constructed with donations from some of the artists or their 'patrons.' The college was incorporated in 1961."

"I take it she died recently."

"About two years ago. At first, there was some opposition from the college's governing board when her half brother, Mark Sutter, wanted to assume control, but after it was all settled, he took over—this past January, as a matter of fact. He doesn't know much about art, but he knows what he likes, and what he likes is profitability."

So we were back to the bottom line again. No wonder Huberman was worried about the future of Pacific Arts. It was hard to imagine people whose eyes filled with dollar signs in the midst of such scenic splendor. As we continued north, the landscape turned bucolic again. Sheep and horses grazed next to fences built close to the road, and the road itself became narrower and more winding. The sun darted in and out through the massive redwoods and eucalyptus lining the twisting highway. Our pace was slowed by a huge logging truck laden with redwood logs, some logs nearly two feet in diameter, others barely eight inches.

Making another stab at small talk, I said, "It doesn't seem like those small trees would yield even a decent two by four."

Meredith shrugged. "Probably not, but often the loggers have to take smaller trees to get to the giants. And some of those logs are just the tops of bigger ones. They can taper a lot up top."

The trip continued in silence for another few miles, past coastal meadows only sparsely dotted with trees. The extended view these open areas allowed revealed the foothills of the Coast Mountain Range.

"You're quite a way from town." I remarked. "It must be hard living alone so far out."

Meredith said nothing, but suddenly turned off the highway onto a side road. The dust the 4x4 kicked up made me close the window on my side, but Meredith just squinted a bit to protect her eyes and kept going. At one point, she hit the brakes abruptly and I looked to see if there was an obstruction in the road. A line of long-necked, full-breasted birds only slightly larger than robins waddled in front of the Explorer like self-important magistrates.

With a grin, Meredith said, "Some of our other residents, Alix. Meet the California quail. Note their little pinheads. It's almost as if they forget they can fly out of harm's way."

We both chuckled, and I was relieved to see that Meredith did have a sense of humor. About a half-mile inland, Meredith turned again, this time onto a narrow gravel driveway. My eyes were still adjusting to the shade produced by the thick canopy of redwood branches overhead, when Meredith again braked suddenly. This time it wasn't a line of native fowl.

"What the hell? Who's that?" she muttered.

Parked across the end of the drive blocking her entry was an ancient white Chevy pickup truck with a yellow Labrador retriever pacing back and forth in the truck bed. Meredith jumped down from her seat and stomped toward the old truck. The big dog stopped pacing to eye her cautiously, but didn't move toward her or make a sound.

"Hey, buddy, whoever you are, move this rusting hulk before I call the sheriff about a trespasser."

I saw a movement behind her and instinctively shouted, "Meredith, look out!" as I dove out of the car and scrambled around the front to stand beside her.

She whirled and came face to face with a dark-haired man coming from the wooded plot next to the driveway. He moved slowly and stopped about three feet in front of her. A stubble of heavy, grey-streaked beard masked some of his features, but he was obviously agitated. He wore stained khaki pants and a blue work shirt, and on his belt was a small leather case with a snap closure. The hilt of a knife peeked through the opening.

"Name's Parisi, *Miss* Coates, you remember me, don't ya? I own the marina and bait shop down in the harbor. You been tryin' to buy me out for a long time now. I just come from a meetin' of the zoning commission where your fancy partner talked about the 'historical significance' of Noyo Harbor."

Fiercely, Meredith snapped, "And you ended up here? Man, are you lost! The harbor's fifteen miles down the coast."

As the man stepped closer to tower over Meredith, I moved in, too, hoping my height, which was about the same as his, would intimidate him a bit. He barely looked in my direction. I wasn't sure how much help I could be, but sometimes presenting a united front is enough. "Think you're pretty funny, don't ya, lady. You'll be laughin' through a lot of busted teeth if you don't keep your hands off this harbor."

It was Meredith's turn to close in on Parisi. She pointed her finger, almost touching his shirt with each jab. "How I make money is my business. If your neighbors want to sell their dilapidated shacks and bankrupt businesses, you've got no say in it."

"Look, bitch," Parisi spat, "I ain't against my neighbors makin' a buck. I jest ain't gonna stand for the likes of you turnin' a working harbor into some candy-ass tourist trap with junk shops and fussy little 'boo-tiques' for queers to hang out."

I looked at Meredith, but she didn't need any help from me. Her already ruddy complexion was florid with anger as she snarled, "Get off my land now. I have no intention of being threatened by you or anyone else. Martin Foster and I have presented our case. I presume you and your friends have done the same. Now it's in the hands of the zoning commission. Whatever they decide, we'll all have to live with it."

Parisi stood his ground for another few seconds, then turned toward the cab of his truck, dragging his left leg a little. Before flinging himself in, he glared back at Meredith. "We'll see who lives with what if you wreck my business, or move out my people."

With a screech of tires, Parisi backed his truck out of the way, spitting gravel, as Meredith smoothed the creases of her navy blue slacks to show her nonchalance. She climbed back into her car, while I waited in the front yard so she could pull into the carport attached to the house. She jumped out and stood with her hands on her hips, glaring at Parisi's truck disappearing down the driveway, the yellow dog still roaming the confines of the truck bed.

The air seemed heavy with the animosity the two had exchanged. I followed Meredith silently and watched as she unlocked her front door. Despite the fearless stand she had made, her hands trembled slightly as she fumbled with the key. I had known this woman less than an hour and already knew some of her enemies. One a petulant, scheming academic; the other a desperate, possibly dangerous working man. How many others might there be?

"Sit down," Meredith said, waving vaguely at a long white wicker sofa with dark blue upholstery. "I'll be back in a minute. Have to meet someone for dinner after my last class, and this is the only chance I've got to change clothes." She disappeared into another room, but I could hear her voice faintly in what was obviously a one-sided conversation on the phone. Windows the length and almost the height of the room made it bright, rather like a sun porch. But it was furnished more substantially with a grey and white dining table and matching white chairs at one end, the sofa and several comfortable-looking armchairs at the other. A machine-made rug with a Native American motif covered the floor in the dining area, while the sitting area sported a couple of throw rugs over a ceramic-tiled floor. The back of the wicker sofa creaked a bit as I rested my head on it. It had been a long day already.

A few moments later Meredith appeared with a tray bearing two stemmed glasses, a carafe of what looked like white wine and a bottle of sparkling water. She had changed into a long-sleeved green pullover and dark grey wool slacks. As she set the tray on the coffee table in front of me, our eyes met. "I'm sorry about that little scene out there. Pete Parisi is the original immovable object. I've been trying to get him to put his place on the market for almost a year. Failing in that, I'm finding people interested in buying up the stores around him."

I shrugged. "What for? If they're as rundown as you said to him, why bother?"

Settling across from me in an easy chair, Meredith gestured toward the carafe, but I shook my head and poured a glass of the sparkling water, while she helped herself to the wine. "Most of those places are falling apart because the owners can't afford to fix them up. Under new owners, with a reasonable amount of capital, they could be turned into something."

Trying not to sound judgmental, I asked, "Something like tourist shops and boutiques?"

Meredith sighed, barely containing her exasperation, "Fishing's almost dead in the harbor. That's not my fault. They can blame the damn federal government, corporate polluters, the farmers in the valley who get most of the water, or the insatiable behemoth that Los Angeles has become that gets the rest of it. But, goddammit, they can't blame me. They're trying to hang onto a past that's just that, the past. There will never be another boom season for salmon, crab, anything." Meredith slapped at the arm of her chair, but the soft fabric made the gesture a silent one.

"I'm just trying to give them a fair price for their property and turn a profit at the same time." She lowered her voice and smiled a little, as if I was someone she needed to persuade to her side. "Look at Nantucket or any other fishing village that's been spared by historic preservation. It's not against the law to earn a decent living." Setting down her wine glass with a soft thud, Meredith said, "Sorry. You're the newcomer. I didn't mean to give you the soapbox lecture. By the way, thanks for backing me up out there with Parisi. You came on pretty strong yourself."

Recalling my plunge down a set of escalator steps last year, I said quietly, "I've had someone come at me from behind. Mainly I wanted to give you an extra pair of eyes. He was pretty angry. But I guess I'm trying to understand his side a little. It's hard to face up to change, to knowing that things can't ever be the way they once were."

Meredith looked at me sharply. "You're not talking about real estate now, are you?"

"No," I admitted, reluctant to let this woman see my vulnerable side. Despite my best effort, my chin trembled once or twice before I regained control. I refused to start crying here in a stranger's house.

Meredith slid over from the chair to a spot next to me on the sofa in a single move. She didn't touch me, but put her hand next to mine as if ready to offer comfort if I needed it. "What's changed for you, Alix? A lover, maybe?" Her voice was soft now, more tender than I could have imagined possible from the woman who had stared down Pete Parisi.

I shook my head. "No, not really. I *was* seeing someone before I left Iowa, but we hadn't been together very long. I guess I was thinking about my friend, Brian, who died."

Meredith leaned back, putting some distance between us again. "I'm sorry, Alix. It's none of my business. I'm at loose ends, myself. I had hoped my partner, Leah, would be up here by now. When I started teaching at Pacific back in January, I bought this place because I refuse to throw good money after bad with rent." As if trying to reassert her business nature, she added quickly, "And the price was right in this economy. She loved this area when we vacationed here, and agreed to come up on weekends until she could wrap up her job in San Francisco." Her voice betrayed hurt and anger when she added, "Unfortunately, that hasn't happened yet."

I wasn't sure I wanted to delve into this woman's personal life, but if Huberman's assessment of the rental housing market was accurate, her cabin might be my best chance for a place to live that wasn't a motel room. And since I don't like surprises at home any more than I do at work, I asked, tentatively, "When was she up here last?"

A mask of indifference fell over Meredith's face. "She had a long weekend over the Fourth of July. She brought up a stack of boxes, some winter clothes and other stuff. The boxes were barely unpacked when we argued. She left Saturday afternoon. Since then it's been tense phone calls and more broken promises."

Eight months seemed like a long time to "wrap up things" on any job. "What kind of work does Leah do?"

"She's a free-lance fund-raiser—organizes people to put together celebrity charity events, hits up corporate sponsors, writes grants for nonprofit groups: schools, museums, special projects, even the tree-huggers."

"Tree-huggers?"

Meredith waved her hand dismissively. "You know, save-the-whales, the redwoods, the owls types. Environmentalists, confirmed no-growth-ers. The job she's been on for the last year or so is for one of the Bay Area zoos. She's raising funds to improve their habitats, trying to turn them into cageless quarters."

I was beginning to understand what they might have fought about. "I see. And you haven't been able to get down to the Bay Area to see her?"

Meredith's eyes were cool again. "It's tough. I've had a lot of meetings lately, and weekends, especially long, holiday weekends, are the hottest times to show property. I've got to keep my hand in the market. God knows I couldn't live on the salary from the college."

Curiosity outweighed caution as I poked a little more into Meredith's story. "How did you two meet?"

She smiled at the memory. "I was running a branch office of Greenspan Realty in San Francisco. Leah made an appointment and came to see me about funding a group that wanted to study the feasibility of turning the Presidio in San Francisco into a national monument when the Army abandons it." Meredith's eyes glazed over slightly, and, almost in a whisper, she added, "That was four years ago, and, for the record, she got what she came for."

I was impressed. Leah must be very persuasive to have gotten that kind of support from Meredith, who clearly had an intolerance for public access to choice land. Or maybe Meredith had been looking to buy more than an environmental study with her contribution.

Meredith moved closer to me on the sofa, and I felt her breath in my hair. I couldn't tell if she was making a pass at me to spite Leah or if she was just lonely. Either way, I'd exposed as much as I dared to this woman. If I took her cabin, payment would come only in hard currency.

Luckily, some distance away a clock chimed three. I checked my watch and said, "Didn't you say you had a four o'clock class? If I'm going to look at your cabin, we'd better do it soon."

We left the sunny sitting room through the front door and walked around the house toward the back of her land. As I followed her down the stone path to the cabin, a tortoiseshell cat with bulging sides darted out and rubbed against her ankles.

"Looks like you're about to have an addition to the family," I called to her back.

"She's not mine, but she seems to have adopted this place as home. I wasn't feeding her or encouraging her at all until I realized she was pregnant. I figured she might have a hard time getting by in her condition so I've been leaving out kibble for the last week or so." After a moment of perfunctory scratching around the ears, the cat took off again.

The cabin stood about a hundred yards from the house. It was a long, narrow rectangle, but a high-sloped roof with two south-facing skylights suggested it would be bright. Inside it was one large, all-purpose room. As Meredith stepped aside to let me survey the space, she said, "The former owner used this as a vacation rental. But I don't have the time to cater to pairs of lovebirds looking for some kind of 'rustic experience.' " The bed, which was situated under one of the skylights, took up most of the far end of the room. Near the bed a small wood-burning stove was perched on a three-foot square brick hearth. "That puts out quite a lot of heat for its size," Meredith said rather proudly.

A worn formica-topped counter led to a new but tiny range, a double stainless-steel sink and one tall cupboard for storage. Behind the front door an old, clunky-looking refrigerator completed the kitchen. Meredith shrugged. "I thought about getting a modern fridge, but this one still works fine, and now I don't know how much longer I'm going to hang onto the property."

"Oh, are you thinking of selling?" Maybe Huberman didn't have to worry about Meredith Coates 'ruining' Pacific Arts after all.

Meredith's voice rose slightly, her tone carried a hint of boasting. "I've got a couple of irons in the fire. If the right commissions and boards approve some plans, alter the zoning regs, that kind of thing, I might move on."

Meredith was thoughtful for a moment. "It's more likely that the commission's decisions, if they rule in my favor, will be challenged by the latest environmental group. And I'll be tied up for years in legal wrangling. They spring up like weeds, choking out as much growth as they can." Meredith laughed at her own analogy as she pulled open a door near the foot of the bed. "This is the bathroom, and that door next to the sink leads to a combination clothes and linen closet. Sorry, there's only a commode and a sink in here. I was planning to expand the cabin, but things got complicated. Leah's the one with building skills anyway. But you'll find a good, hot shower on the deck."

"The deck?" I said, incredulously.

She led me out to show me the shower. A fancy pulsating showerhead bent down from a length of exposed PVC pipe, tacked to the side of the cabin with U-shaped braces. Next to the shower was a redwood shelf with several small indentations carved out for soap, shampoo and other toiletries. Two thick brass hooks were attached to the siding. I presumed one was for towels, the other for a robe or clothes.

"With the redwoods so close and thick, it's absolutely private. Weather here is very mild, but if we did get a cold snap, you'd be welcome to use one of the showers in the main house. Hell, since this one's heated by propane and is gravity-fed, you might even find me out here lathering up, if we have a power outage. My place is all-electric," she said with mocking pride. A derisive tone crept into her voice as she added, "and utterly useless if one of the power lines gets knocked down in a storm." Almost as an afterthought she added, "Since you're faculty here, I'd let you have it for $250 a month."

When I was silent, she said, a little regretfully, "Maybe this is a little too primitive for your tastes. I can understand..."

"No, it's alright," I said, not willing to be considered a wimp. "I was just surprised." After an awkward pause, I asked, "Can I think about this a bit, maybe give you a call tomorrow, or the day after?"

Meredith shrugged again to hide her disappointment. "Sure, anytime before Monday's fine. That's the deadline for putting an ad in the weekly paper. I guess it is time we started back. Why don't you wait for me in the car?"

Climbing into Meredith's 4x4, I admired the stable feel of the substantial vehicle, and thought, *Something like this wouldn't get blown all over the road like the VW.* I was still sizing up the car, inspecting the instruments in the dashboard when I heard, "Hi. You a friend of Meredith's?"

I looked out and down at a woman peering into the car. She was small, probably in her late thirties, and her blonde hair seemed too perfect not to come out of a bottle. Her expression was tense, almost hostile.

Startled at being crept up on, I stammered, "Um, well, I just met her today. We're about to be colleagues over at Pacific Arts."

The belligerent glare remained in her flat green eyes, but a dry smirk twisted her mouth. "Met her today, and already comin' home with her. For what? A drink? A lunch time quickie? Works fast, that woman."

I was so stunned I almost couldn't close my mouth to form a reply, but I finally managed to gather up some proper indignation. "Now, wait a minute...I don't even know your name, nor you mine, and you're making a hell of a lot of assumptions."

Waving her hand at me nonchalantly, the woman said, "Chill, lady. Just teasing. But don't tell me you're not the type. This place," she said with a wide, vague gesture, "...a goddammed magnet for you dykes."

I was tired, confused by all the personal and political intrigues I'd stepped into in the last few hours. And more than a little annoyed at this woman for her attitude and her seeming inability to form complete sentences. "I see. And do you make a habit of being rude to people you don't know?"

Looking ever so slightly contrite, the woman replied, "You're right. Meredith and I are pals, but that don't give me the right to needle her other friends. Sorry." She reached up and stuck her hand through the open car window. "Veronica Battles. Been a summer and weekend resident here about five years. My husband, Bert and I, own the house across the road. I lost my job last spring, so just now I'm, ah, sort of 'at liberty.' No need hangin' around that crowded, dirty city. Bert can just damn well take care of himself down there. Spends most of his time in that damn union office, anyway."

I was about to introduce myself when the screen door slammed on the porch, and Meredith ambled down the stairs, her Western boots tapping sharply against the weathered wood. "Vernie, are you has-sling my new friend Alix? When are you going to learn not everyone appreciates your brand of humor? Back off, will ya? I'm trying to get her to rent the cabin. I could use the help with the mortgage."

Wariness sprang back into Veronica Battles's eyes as she said, "Oh, so you might become a neighbor. Alix, was it?"

I nodded slightly at Veronica. "Alix Nicholson, and I'm think-ing about the cabin; I haven't decided. It *is* kind of small." *And this neighborhood is getting awfully small for the three of us*, I thought.

Meredith eased herself behind the wheel. "See you later, Vernie. Alix needs to get back to her car, and I've got a bunch of eager young entrepreneurs to teach this afternoon."

When we were out of the driveway, Meredith patted me lightly on the thigh then put her hand back on the wheel. I couldn't decide if she was just the type to get familiar in a friendly sort of way quickly, or if she was making a second-rate pass. "Don't let Veronica get to you. She thinks that all lesbians talk or think about is sex. But Bert Battles is secretary-treasurer of Local 485 of the Ship Welders Union down in Oakland. Now he's aiming at a regional position and has a strong opponent for the election." Meredith shook her head, and there was a look of pity in her eyes. "She's so neglected by that ambitious husband of hers that all she can do is talk about it. It's no wonder Vernie took the opportunity after her layoff to spend some time away from him. Maybe she was hoping he would start to miss her, but the way she talks, I suspect he encouraged her coming up here."

Meredith turned to catch my eyes, adding, "She's even come on to me a time or two." Her gaze returned to the road as she finished, "But I'm not about to get tangled up with a 'lesbo-tourist' looking for a little recreation and a way to make her husband jealous."

"She said you were friends."

Meredith shrugged. "I guess we are in a way. Leah and I met her about two years ago when we were the couple staying in the love nest for ten days. But she's terribly needy. Remember the old 'tarbaby' story? That's how I feel about Vernie. Get too close, and you'll have a hell of a time getting free."

Meredith had rather accurately described how I was beginning to feel about every aspect of this new environment. I thought I had prepared myself for living in a small town again, but suddenly it all seemed very taxing. Clearly, Huberman expected me to be an ally in his struggle to protect Pacific Arts, and Veronica Battles seemed to view me as some kind of competition for Meredith's time and attention. And what of Meredith and her partner, Leah? The accusation Meredith had aimed at Veronica Battles had already entered my mind, but in my scenario, Meredith was the pursuer and I was the bait to make Leah jealous. What were the odds of being able to steer clear of their troubles if I was living less than a football field's length from their house, and possibly dropping in for the occasional shower to boot?

"You and Leah stayed in the cabin before you owned this place?"

Softly Meredith said, "Yes. I knew she liked this area. I thought it would help..." Her voice drifted off to silence.

Leaning back to take in the magnificent ocean gliding by my window, I resolved to make a serious effort to find other housing arrangements before stepping voluntarily into this possible quagmire.

By Sunday afternoon, I was resigned to taking Meredith's offer of the rental cabin despite the tangle of issues I'd be living with. A dozen phone calls and three forays out to look at places had left me feeling either underpaid or just plain rejected. Most of the available rentals were out of my price range, and some of the other landlords refused to talk to me after learning I'd be leaving the area right after the holidays. The worst time, they claimed, to try and find another acceptable tenant. One place that was about to become vacant got scratched off the list when the renter refused to let me see it while she was still there. The agent was annoyed that I wouldn't sign a lease sight unseen.

Two possibilities I did look at were as small as Meredith's cabin, but without the amenities hers possessed. One had running water, but only for washing; the outhouse was a hundred feet from the back door. The other was just dark and depressing.

While practicing not sounding desperate, I sat on my bed in the motel room, punched in Meredith's number and waited. Somehow I imagined her trying not to sound triumphant as she said, "Alix, I was wondering if I'd hear from you. Of course, it's still available. I said I'd give you the weekend. You can move in tonight if you'd like."

I was not about to appear *that* desperate. "No, Tuesday's fine. This room's paid for until then, and I really wanted to spend this evening working on an opening presentation to my classes."

"Suit yourself, woman. I'll see you on Tuesday up here. It doesn't sound like our schedules are going to coincide much. Too bad, we could have carpooled."

It was a small thing to be grateful for, but I was glad the school schedule would allow me some moments of utter solitude. *There you go again, Nicholson. Solitude, tranquility, peace—whatever you try to call it, you're becoming a goddammed loner.*

With all my equipment and clothes packed back into the van, I headed north from the motel Tuesday afternoon, contemplating the semester I had signed up for. Despite the fact that there was a prerequisite of a beginning photo class, a couple of students in the documentary class had gotten a waiver from the registrar, or possibly from Huberman, himself, because they needed an art credit that fit into their schedule. I wasn't sure they knew which end of the camera to look through, much less how to load a nonautomatic 35 mm. Two of the others were gadget freaks who each had an array of lenses, filters, flash attachments, strobe lights ad infinitum. But I wasn't convinced they cared about telling a story with their pictures. Mainly, they wanted the use of the darkroom space until their credit cards cooled off enough to support the next round of equipment purchases.

My enthusiasm about this "opportunity" was ebbing fast, and I was beginning to think my luck was not that great after all. But with the afternoon sun streaming through my car window, warming my face and neck, I found myself almost leaning into it for the heat. At least that was still a plus for the North Coast. I reminded myself that within a few short weeks, the early snowstorms that often preceded the start of winter could blow into Iowa. I'd be slip-sliding all over icy highways in this little van, if it weren't for the job out here.

Standing outside Meredith's front door, I pulled down a note addressed to me. "Last minute errand in town. Go on in and make yourself comfortable. Back soon." Despite the invitation, I felt like an intruder stepping into Meredith's home in her absence. I considered waiting politely in the sun room for her to return, but my natural inquisitiveness got the better of me. Taking pictures of people in their own milieu was a good way to learn something about them. As I strolled through the rooms downstairs, I tried to envision Meredith at ease in them.

The kitchen was pristine: eggshell-white walls with a black marbled countertop and modern appliances that matched the color of the walls. Light oak cabinets supported the countertop and hung above it. But it seemed too perfect. There were no utensils or small appliances sitting out for easy access, no dishes in the sink, nothing out of place. Perhaps she was simply a tidy person, but I suspected that it went deeper than that. To Meredith, everything had some kind of price. As much as she seemed to enjoy her home, it was ready to show at the drop of an offer.

The doorway from the kitchen led into a more formal sitting room than the sun room at the front of the house. It was dominated by a rough grey stone fireplace flanked by seven-foot-high redwood bookcases. The furnishings, too, were more substantial, but the love seat, two side chairs and area rug echoed Meredith's apparent liking of the popular Southwestern motifs. The colors evoked sandstone and washed-out rose sunsets. The drapes, in a pale turquoise and tan pattern, completed the look.

Beyond the sitting room, I could see an open staircase and considered going up. But that *did* seem intrusive. Wandering through the rooms where people normally received visitors was one thing. Stepping into someone's bedroom was altogether different.

Hoping something in the bookcases would offer a diversion for my curiosity, I scanned the selections idly, expecting Meredith to show up any minute. The books about self-made millionaires and long-term investing didn't appeal to me at all, but they added a piece to the puzzle of Meredith Coates and what drove her.

On one of the lower shelves, I found a book with an older collection of poetry by Adrienne Rich, but it slipped out of my hands as I pulled it out. As I stooped to retrieve it from the floor, a familiar spine caught my eye on the bottom shelf. There, arranged chronologically by publication dates I knew well, was a complete set of the five documentary photo books I'd had published.

Could Meredith have been the mysterious person who showed Huberman my work and prompted my invitation from the art department? Somehow I doubted it. The way Meredith selected the things she lived with demonstrated a sophisticated taste in design and color, but nothing on the walls or in her conversation indicated she had an appreciation of art. Nor, I presumed, would her endorsement carry much weight with Huberman. I pulled out one of the books to see if it had a stamp or library mark, but there was no identifying clue.

I returned the copy of my work to the shelf and settled down with the book of poetry. I felt a need to taste the wisdom and clarity in Rich's lyrics to ease my growing confusion.

Moments later I heard the rumble of Meredith's heavy car pulling into the driveway. Before I could decide whether or not to ask her about my books, she was in the room. She wore a tailored grey shirt with a button-down collar, pressed navy blue slacks and Rockport walking shoes that matched her slacks. The tight creases in the slacks made her seem taller than the five foot three or four I guessed her to be. A black bolo tie held a silver slide with an etched coyote head at her neckline. She seemed almost elegant, and made me feel underdressed in my black cotton pullover shirt and faded jeans that were too short for my long legs.

"Good!" Her voice boomed in the quiet house. "I'm glad you took me at my word. Sorry I wasn't here earlier, but someone called from the title office in town about papers I needed to fax to my lawyer."

I tried to shrug off her absence. "It was no problem, I..."

"Yes, I see you found something in Leah's stash of books."

"Leah's?"

"The poetry, fiction, art books, everything on the two bottom shelves. They're all hers."

Putting down the poetry collection, I got up and went to the bookcases. I pulled out one of my books and held it out to Meredith. "Including these?"

Meredith took the book from me with a surprised look. "Why, yes. You know, I never made the connection. I haven't looked much at her stuff lately. She used to bring boxes of her stuff up every time she came." Holding the book lightly, almost fondling the cover, she added, "It made me think she really meant it when she said she'd be moving up after her job with the zoo was done."

With a thoughtful tone, Meredith nodded in my direction. "Now I remember. The weekend before spring vacation we had a faculty party out here. Leah brought several boxes of books up. She stayed the rest of the week, and we drove to Vancouver Island for spring break. I thought things were going to work out for us then."

The sadness in Meredith's face told me she now had little hope of "things working out" between her and Leah. I was a little uncomfortable at Meredith's frequent and detailed accounts of her personal and business relationships. She knew almost nothing about me, and I knew far more than I wanted to at this stage about her. I appreciated her pain, but I was still curious about Leah's possible connection to my ending up in Fort Bragg. "Was Roald Huberman at the faculty party?"

"Rollie? Yes, I suppose he was. It's a pretty small faculty, and we try to be civil when we can. Why do you...?" Meredith looked down at the book in her hands. "You mean you think this was the first he saw of your work?"

Shaking my head, I admitted, "I don't know, Meredith. He never told me where he first saw my documentary work. I've been meaning to ask him, but I guess I'm reluctant to acknowledge that my stuff has very limited distribution. Maybe if Huberman's primary discipline was photography, I'd buy that he'd found my work on his own, but he's a watercolorist. And from what I saw the other day, and from some of the students he let into my advanced class, I'd guess he doesn't know a lot about photography."

Laying the book on a side table, Meredith shrugged. "Beats me. I don't even remember Leah talking to Huberman that evening. And I'd bet, if you asked Rollie, he'd have trouble remembering Leah's name. He can be extremely vague on some things. Anyway what difference does it make? You're here now. You aren't sorry, are you?"

Conceding that it didn't make any difference, I asked Meredith about a lease for the cabin.

"Lease? I don't think that's necessary, do you?" Stepping a little closer to me, she looked up at me with a smile that erased the sad, puzzled look. "How about just a handshake, a handshake over dinner? I've got a couple of steaks in the freezer, and it's still warm enough to barbecue outdoors."

I opened my mouth to object, both to dinner and to leaving our rental contract an intangible verbal agreement. But more than anything, I wanted to be settled. After almost two weeks on the road trying to be a fun-loving sightseer, and another week in the motel room in Fort Bragg, I longed for a place to spread out my things and to call my space. Hoping a small concession now would mean an amiable relationship for the duration of my stay, I nodded. "Sounds good. What can I do to help?" And in the back of my mind, another question lingered. *What are the chances of meeting this woman who seems to know my work?*

As I stood under the prickly shower and gazed out at the massive redwoods dark with early morning mist, I had to admit it was a joyous way to start the day. I breathed in the spicy forest scents and admired the deep greens and browns of the sheltering trees. And Meredith had been right about the temperature. It was now the middle of October, and there was a morning chill in the air, but it was easily chased off by the hot mist of the shower. In the four weeks since I'd taught my first class at Pacific Arts and moved into the cabin behind Meredith's house, I'd fallen into a routine designed to maintain friendly relations both here and at school, while keeping my distance from potentially difficult situations.

I hadn't heard any more about Meredith's plans to "take over" or "sell-out" Pacific Arts and the fine arts department from under Huberman. His more pressing concern seemed to be the federal and state budgets, especially in light of the right-wing attack on grants from the National Endowment for the Arts in Washington. The school administration was being forced to consider program and salary cuts and/or hefty tuition increases. Either could hurt the school in a variety of ways.

Veronica Battles was keeping a low profile, too. We had exchanged waves and a few words a couple of times, but I'd apparently proved an unworthy object for either her humor or her ardor.

The only dark cloud was Pete Parisi, who seemed to be dogging Meredith's trail. Although he had not shown up on the property to threaten Meredith again, I had seen his old truck parked along Highway 1 near the turnoff to the house on a couple of occasions, and I'd noticed it in the college parking lot close to Meredith's Explorer.

The first time I mentioned having seen his truck, Meredith shrugged off any danger, saying, "Pete can talk a lot of shit, but I doubt he's got the balls to try anything."

The next time I saw the old white Chevy truck sitting in close proximity to Meredith's car in the school's lot, I was returning from a field trip with my class. My Nikon was slung on my shoulder so I raised the viewfinder to my eye and snapped a few shots, making sure to get two that included both Parisi's truck and Meredith's car. At least if Meredith did finally take Parisi seriously, she'd have some proof he was tailing her.

As part of my noninvolvement tactic, I had politely declined subsequent dinner invitations from Meredith, although occasionally I felt a little guilty doing so. Meredith, for all her powers of persuasion and dreams of wealth, was essentially a lonely woman, possibly as lonely and rejected as she contended Veronica Battles was. To defuse the rejections, I'd invited her out to the cabin for coffee a few weekend mornings, and for a glass of wine one evening in the middle of the second week.

I had barely slipped back into the cabin after a shower and was throwing on a my thick blue terry cloth robe when I heard first the click of her boots on the deck, then a rap on the door.

"Good morning! I brought some fresh apple bread from the bakery."

Making sure my robe belt was snugly tied, I opened the door. "Good morning to you. Kind of early, isn't it?"

Meredith's eyelids were puffy possibly from lack of sleep, but there was a brightness in her eyes. "Come on out. I want to show you something," she said excitedly. I looked down at my attire, but she laughed, "Nah, don't worry about it. Who's to see?"

Trailing Meredith, I stepped off the cabin deck into the dewy grass. She motioned me to follow her around the cabin. On the south side, a shallow woodshed held a supply of firewood cut to fit the cabin's stove. Meredith pointed to a corner of the shed where a small pile of twigs and leaves had been scratched into a nest.

I looked down to find the old tortoiseshell now gaunt and unkempt, lying on her side nursing a single orange and white kitten less than two weeks old. At our approach, she raised her head and eyed us warily, but her paws still kneaded the air and her purr was loud.

"Crafty old broad, isn't she?" Meredith said. As she looked at the pair, her face was transformed from the tough, shrewd money-maker, and became almost childlike. "Not only did she pick the warmest, most sheltered spot around, but when she needs to hunt, there should be plenty of mice and voles and lizards scurrying around this woodpile."

We watched the mother and infant scene for a few moments, then I began to feel the cool air on my barely covered body. Feeling tender toward this new, exposed aspect of Meredith, I linked my arm in hers and said, "How about some coffee to go with that apple bread? I should be getting dressed."

As we came back around the cabin, we ran smack into Veronica Battles who glared at me openly. "Out for a little stroll, are we?"

Meredith slipped her arm out of mine and shrugged nonchalantly. "I was just showing Alix that I found the tortie. She finally dropped her litter. Just one kitten, but she's pretty old and had a tough life. That's probably enough for her to handle."

Veronica's gaze had lost some of its heat, but it was still fixed on me. "Maybe you should contact animal control and have them get rid of the things before they overrun the place."

Meredith laughed, but her voice was edgy. "That's what most of the locals say about my clients who are buying land up here. That cat has the right to raise this kitten until it's at least up and around. Then maybe I'll see about having the Humane Society pick them up and try to find homes for them."

"Suit yourself," Veronica said, turning on her heel. She disappeared down the wooded path back to her house, and Meredith relaxed visibly.

Back in the cabin, I brought plates and a bread knife to the table and sat down across from her. We drank coffee and nibbled at the slices of bread in silence for a few minutes, Meredith shifting uncomfortably in the old straight-backed chair, fussing with the open collar of her crisp white shirt. She noticed my look at her flitting hands and said, "Can't seem to make this collar stand up right. I usually wear a bolo tie with this, but I couldn't find it this morning." After a pause, she slapped the tops of her khaki-clad thighs, and said, "I need to get going. I've got some things I need to do today, and this evening there's a potluck party up at the Spread. You know, this is the first gathering since you came to the Coast. Come with me and meet some of the women's community."

"The Spread?" I asked.

"Yes, it's quite a holding. Almost 250 acres, mostly along the southern bank of the Mandarin River. There are numerous cabins and converted barns on the land, plus a falling-down old mansion. Only women can stay on the Spread; it was written into the will left by Isaac Winters. Most of them are lesbians, like Willow, but not all."

I looked at Meredith questioningly. "Willow?"

"Willow Shade was his first tenant, and she became the manager in 1986 when he died. The party's for her birthday, but no one knows which birthday."

Meredith looked at me as if she knew I was about to beg off, and added, "And don't think you wouldn't be welcome. They're a very tolerant bunch. Why, they even let me in even though they hate the things I'm trying to do to 'grow' this burg into a viable town."

I started to decline, but the truth was that, despite the acquaintances I had made among the other artists on staff at Pacific, I had been missing contact with dykes. The almost instant recognition, the easy banter as if we were all getting the same joke at the same time...these were feelings possible only among sisters. "I'll come," I said finally. "But maybe we should drive separately in case you want to stay longer, or..."

"Nah, don't worry about it. I'm not much for hanging around late at these things." With some derision in her voice, she added, "Sometimes they get a little obscure for me, lapsing into spiritual stuff— you know, chanting, lighting candles, ringing bells."

"You don't sound like you care much for these women."

Meredith smiled almost to herself. "I guess I do come off that way. They're all okay. Better than okay—funny, bright, talented women. They just settle for so little. They own almost nothing, even the cars they drive are falling apart. And yet every time you turn around, they're thanking some goddess or another, being grateful for what the spirits have given them. I like them, I just don't get them." Meredith's voice dropped, and her eyes seemed to look far away. With a deep sigh, she got up. "Forget everything I've said, Alix. They're good women, and you should form your own opinions. Their ceremonies and rituals are often quite beautiful, even moving. I've got no business passing judgment on them. Not after the way I've screwed up.... Never mind."

Taking a final swig of coffee that was probably cold, Meredith just said "Seven o'clock" and waved goodbye. As I cleared away the coffee and bread, I started thinking about an appropriate potluck dish to bring for people I'd never met.

The Spread really was spectacular. Sitting high on a bluff about five miles south of the town of Westport, the small houses, cabins and outbuildings dotted the landscape as far as the eye could see. A few contented sheep grazed near the old main house, ignoring the feisty little dog that raced between them as if she were running an obstacle race. Looking back toward the highway as Meredith pointed her 4x4 up the drive, I could see the narrow river widen as it swept under the bridge and out to sea. It gratified me to think that only women had the privilege of that sight on a daily basis.

A woman as tall as I, with shoulder-length, snow-white hair and broad, square shoulders, strode toward us as we got out of the car. Her slim hips and legs were clad in soft, well-worn jeans, topped by a red, yellow and black Mexican-style pullover shirt, the kind with a hood in the back and a pouch-type pocket across the front. She patted Meredith on the arm playfully. "Still trying to sell off the whole town, woman?"

"The town and anything else anyone is willing to let me put on the market," Meredith grinned. "Hey, thanks for hanging around to have another birthday. I'd like you to meet my tenant, Alix Nicholson. Alix, this is the notorious Willow Shade."

I looked up into the gentlest-looking grey eyes I'd ever seen, set in a narrow tanned face, which was well-lined from a lifetime of smiles and frowns. A generous thatch of white facial hair curled under her chin, and I found myself thinking, *What a beautiful face.* Extending my hand, I said almost shyly, "Glad to meet you. Thanks for letting me come to your place."

Shaking her head, Willow said, "Not *my* place. I just look after it 'cause the law in its wisdom says someone's name has to be on the piece of paper that describes this parcel of land." I knew I was going to like this woman right away.

With a snort, she added, "As if anyone really owns the land, we're all jest takin' up space for a time."

Rolling her eyes, Meredith broke in amiably. "Not tonight, you old crone. Take a rest from your soapbox for your birthday."

Willow bowed her head slightly in acquiescence, then tweaked Meredith's ear as if she were a naughty child. "Damn lucky you're a dyke, or I'd have run you off this place the first time you showed up." Willow Shade moved on to greet another group of guests who had just parked their cars.

Together, Meredith and I walked to a long buffet table where I set down a meatless lasagna-type dish that substituted a bean filling for ricotta. Since I had put it together from memory, I hoped it would be tasty as well as politically correct. Most of the women were seated in a circle on folding chairs or blankets spread out on the grass.

After Meredith and I filled our plates with a green salad, couscous with peas and pine nuts, a slice of the lasagna, some cut-up fruit and homemade whole wheat bread, we got drinks and separated to find comfortable spots. My hands were full, so I set down my beer and tucked a plastic fork into the side pocket of the loose-fitting pants I'd bought at a local store featuring Guatemalan fabrics and designs. They were extremely comfortable, and the subtle black and white print went with several of my shirts and tops, including the yellow turtle-neck sweater I'd slipped on after Meredith's warning that evenings turned very cool near the river. I recognized a woman from one of my classes who had told me she was a nurse. She was sitting on a tattered quilt, and I nodded toward a vacant spot next to her, asking if the seat was taken. With a smile, she gestured for me to sit down and introduced me to two other women sharing the quilt, Doris and Sue.

"Do you live out here, Connie?"

"No. I live in town closer to the hospital, but I stay out here sometimes...with Doris." She reached over to squeeze the hand of a young, heavyset, dark-haired woman sitting cross-legged next to her.

Smiling broadly toward Connie, Doris said, "Connie said you might turn out to be one of us. I just reminded her not to enjoy your class too much."

We chuckled together as I made a cross-my-heart gesture about not getting involved with students. It was fun to share that kind of laughter, something only possible when you were teaching adults. For a brief moment my memories hauled me back to my hometown in Missouri, and the uproar created when two of my female students had taken nude pictures of each other and insisted it was a class assignment. "Lesbian recruiter" was the most polite epithet aimed at me; "perverted child molester" was the worst, as if there were any other kind. From the end of that term until this fall, I had not taught any class more than a few weeks at a time as a substitute.

"Alix." Connie called me back to the present. "I don't know if you do any photography outside of your documentary stuff, but there are some great landscapes just a bit upstream. Doris would let you use her canoe sometime, if you're interested."

I thanked them both for their generosity and, silently, for pulling me away from thoughts of the dismal days of my early teaching career.

As darkness set in, some of the women started drifting away, singly or in pairs. I had just said good night to Connie and Doris and was watching them stroll toward Doris's cabin with arms around each other when Meredith appeared above me. Reaching down to help me up, she asked, "Ready to head back home, Alix?"

I agreed it was time to go. In the car on the way back, I thanked Meredith for inviting me. "It was good to feel part of a community again. You and Willow seemed to be good friends, all that teasing about her notoriety and such."

Meredith shrugged, "Willow enjoys making a joke of it, but the truth is, she had a hell of a time after old Mr. Winters died and left the property in trust to her. His only other relatives were a couple of greedy nephews who accused Willow of brainwashing a sick old man. They even hinted she might have hurried his demise to keep him from changing his mind."

Even though it was just history now, I was angry that anyone could vilify an obviously gentle and upright soul like Willow. "Thankfully she won, but I suppose these relatives were surprised that he would put the women-only stipulations in his will."

Meredith let out an explosive snort. "Hah. It didn't take the judge more than five minutes to figure that one out. Winters had only one child, a daughter, Beth. His wife died when she was about eight, and Beth became his whole world. She had just graduated from high school in 1970, and moved to the city to 'live a little' before starting college. She was raped and murdered by a gang of drunken thugs in an alley. Winters had sixteen years to grieve and to see how violent the world had become. Willow says that before he died he swore there'd be some safe place on earth for women."

The weight of all that pain silenced us both for a time, and the only sound was Meredith's powerful vehicle slicing through the darkness. That deep hum and a light fog hovering just above the road like a soft cocoon did make me feel safe and sheltered. As we swung off the highway onto the dirt road, Meredith said, "Thanks for the coffee this morning. I'm sorry if I barged in, but I had to get away from...from Vernie."

"What are you saying, Meredith?"

Her voice thick with self-loathing, Meredith sighed, "I'm saying I talk a good game, but sometimes I can't follow through. I'd almost convinced myself that Leah would never come up here again, and Veronica caught me at a vulnerable time, and it just happened."

Meredith's face in the dim light from the dashboard was morose, the planes deeply etched with shadow. Her jaw tight, she continued, "I started sleeping with her about two months ago. This morning I got back from her place and found a message from Leah. She's coming up next weekend. Now I'm scared shitless that even if Leah wants to try and get back together, Vernie's going to fuck it up with her big mouth."

"I'm sorry you're in such a mess, Meredith. I know how it feels to be lonely." We turned into the long driveway, and I was still looking at Meredith when I felt her slam on the brakes. Luckily we weren't moving very fast because the trunk of a good-sized tree lay across the drive. The Ford's bumper had missed slamming into the tree by a mere couple of inches.

After Meredith set the hand brake, we both jumped out and looked at the trunk. "I didn't think there was much wind tonight," I said, uneasily. "Could this tree have just toppled over, rotted maybe?"

Meredith snatched a flashlight from under the driver's seat and looked closely at the tree. "This tree was alive until just hours ago. Look at the foliage, it's green and supple. And the wood is strong, too." Following the tree trunk into the thicket next to the driveway, we found the end resting next to the stump, a clean saw cut revealing that this was not an act of nature, but of man. But what man?

I looked at Meredith, the harsh glare from the flashlight was reflected in her eyes. "I wonder if Parisi did this to try and scare me. I'm going to have a talk with him first thing tomorrow. He'd better back off if he knows what's good for him."

The car was safely off the road, and it was too late to do anything more about the obstacle tonight. Meredith assured me that she'd have someone out early tomorrow, even though it was a Sunday, to remove the tree so I could get my VW out in time for my Monday morning class. We climbed over the medium-sized trunk and said our good-nights next to her house. I touched her arm briefly. "Good night. Be careful with Parisi. If you want me to go with you, just ask. As for the other stuff, I hope things work out for you and Leah."

She covered my hand with hers. It was icy despite the mild temperatures. "Parisi's my problem, but thanks. And thanks for the good wishes. I'll probably need all I can get."

We turned away from each other, and I walked through the long yard to the cabin. The time we had spent checking around the property, plus the fear that someone was menacing Meredith, made me feel very cold, but I didn't have the energy to start a fire. After brushing my teeth to restore some normalcy to the evening, I quickly stripped off my clothes and huddled under the heavy down comforter. Even the sheets were cold, and I shuddered slightly and felt my nipples tighten in the chill. Touching one nipple then the other, I felt a warmth begin in the center of my body. Clenching my teeth, I opened my vulva and found the moist core of my own desire. As I squeezed my eyes shut, I tried to recall the sweeping vista of the river as it flowed into the ocean, but all I could see was two women walking away from me entangled in each other's arms.

I tried again the following morning to get Meredith to let me go with her to talk to Parisi, but she was adamant. Instead, she asked that I stay at the house to wait for the man who was coming to saw up and move the tree. She left instructions on where he should stack the logs and money to pay him. I felt like I was being given some insignificant task to distract me. "Meredith, this sounds like you're going to be gone all day."

"I've got appointments to show some land this afternoon." When I protested that I was worried about her meeting with Parisi, she laughed, "That fucker may be a couple of inches taller than me, but I can handle Pete in any situation." Her voice softening, she handed me the key to the house. "But thanks for worrying. Go on in and make yourself a pot of coffee. I'll call you from the real estate office after I've seen old Pete. He'll be lucky to still have a 'peter' when I'm done with him."

Other than the tree incident, which Meredith said Parisi had vehemently denied being involved in, the week after the potluck on the Spread had started out well. Being with other lesbians, some living alone and some in loving relationships, had bolstered my spirits and helped me start to look ahead toward my return to Dubuque. I had a lot going for me there: a comfortable, if small house, a community of friends who only wanted the best for me, and a well-equipped darkroom and studio. If I wanted to do other kinds of photography such as weddings and family gatherings, or graduation and class pictures at some of the schools, I could probably even quit substitute teaching. If any of the projects this class was working on got some exposure, I could possibly even pick up other artist-in-residence gigs.

Although my fears that Meredith was being threatened by someone had cost me a lot of my objectivity about her, I tried to maintain a discreet distance from her personal relationship problems. I was tired of getting vile looks from her neighbor, Veronica, who found out we had gone to the party at the Spread together. And as much as I wanted to meet Leah and find out where she first encountered my work, I thought about leaving town before she showed up at the house this coming weekend. I didn't want to be a witness to any of their fireworks.

I was locking up the photo lab late on Thursday afternoon when Dr. Huberman stuck his head out of his classroom, which was down the hall from the lab, and motioned for me to come in. With a sweeping gesture, he offered me a chair. "Please, sit down. I just wanted to tell you that I've heard excellent comments about your classes. The students are very pleased with your methods, and my colleagues who have seen some of the interim prints think the class is making fine progress."

Since the classes had been going on now for nearly six weeks, and this was the first time he had chosen to comment on the work, I wasn't sure what he really wanted. I took the chair he offered, but sat on the edge waiting for his next move. "Thank you. For the most part, the advanced group is a very sharp class. Even the two who received a waiver of prerequisites seem to have caught on rather quickly." My smile was polite, but I suspect even he knew it was artificial. I was still upset that he had not warned me about the novices he'd steered into the accelerated class.

With just a slight flush to his round cheeks, Huberman plucked imaginary threads from the lapel of his lumpy, tan corduroy jacket. "Oh, yes. Those two. I meant to speak with you about them before class started, and I suppose it just slipped my mind. I am glad that it has worked out. They very much needed another class to maintain their full-time status, and well..."

I dismissed his excuse before he could finish. "It's really not important now. They've chosen to work together on an interesting documentary subject down at the harbor, and they're doing fine."

"Good," he said.

I rose to leave, but he stepped just slightly in front of the door to slow my departure. "By the way, have you heard anything about Ms. Coates's partner coming up here to look at property?"

"What?" I immediately thought of Leah, and I wasn't about to share any part of Meredith's personal life with Huberman.

"Her business partner from Sacramento, Martin Foster."

I moved around Huberman and put my hand on the doorknob. The smile was gone from my face and every pretense at politeness was gone. As directly as I knew how, I said through clenched teeth, "Look, Dr. Huberman, I am a tenant in a cabin some distance from Ms. Coates's house. I don't have a habit of spending a lot of time in her company. We are both busy people, and I am really not interested in her real estate dealings. I've come to like Pacific Arts quite a lot, and I would be sorry if it had to fold. But I won't have anything to do with spying on my colleagues."

He looked flustered, but his voice kept its even, monotonous pitch. "No, no, I meant nothing like that. I was just wondering if you knew why she might need a contact in the state capital. And is he really just a partner or is he perhaps a lobbyist? There's quite a lot of competition for educational funding, and if Pacific had some problem, like losing its accreditation, we would have to close rather quickly. While we could technically still operate, our capacity for fundraising would diminish considerably."

I pulled the door open to end the conversation. Lowering my voice to maintain calm, I said, stiffly, "I sympathize with your concerns, Dr. Huberman, I genuinely do. But I neither have nor want any knowledge about Ms. Coates's business deals. Now, if you'll excuse me, I'd really like to get home. I've been here since eight a.m."

By the time I was pulling into the driveway, my anger had dissipated considerably. Even the brief glimpses of ocean had a soothing effect. Now I longed to stretch out on my bed under the skylight with a good book until supper time. Having classes on Monday and Wednesday, with open labs on Thursday, gave me the luxury of a three-day weekend every week. But after today's little brush with Huberman, I really wanted to hibernate, tuck myself away until Monday morning. Apparently, it was not to be, for Meredith was striding away from my cabin. She quickened her pace when she saw me. Her small, well-manicured hand almost obscured the tiny ball of orange fur that was awkwardly snagging her plum-colored mohair sweater.

"You haven't seen the tortie today, have you?" she asked, her voice shrill with concern.

I shook my head. "I've been gone all morning. I know I saw her Tuesday, my day off, when I went to fill the log sling. She even let me pet the kitten for a moment. Its eyes are open now."

"Yeah, I know," she said, looking down at the feebly struggling kitten which was mewing in apparent hunger. "I saw the baby stumbling around outside the woodshed and went to check on her. The mama cat wouldn't let her venture out that far on her own. I picked her up, but I've got to be at school in less than an hour. I don't know quite what to do." Meredith's concerned frown and her almost child-like references to the mother cat and its kitten intrigued me. It seemed so uncharacteristic for this tough-minded business woman.

"You don't suppose she went hunting after something she couldn't handle, do you?" I asked.

"I don't know what to think. I've even considered questioning some of the trouble-making kids in the neighborhood. It's only a little over a week until Halloween. Maybe someone's playing a rotten trick, holding the mama cat, or worse."

Watching Meredith struggle with the helpless baby, I gave up my plans to hide away, at least for the moment. "Why don't we take her inside and see if she can eat anything on her own. That way I can take care of her and keep an eye out for the tortie in case she comes back." I took the little ball of fur and carried her into the cabin with Meredith close behind. Meredith warmed some milk for the kitten while I made a pot of tea. We sat down at the kitchen table, and I dipped my finger in the milk. By rubbing the droplets down her tiny muzzle, I got her tongue working. I fed her that way for a couple of minutes, then gently nudged her toward the shallow saucer on the table. We both breathed sighs of relief when the kitten managed to lap milk from the saucer on her own after only a couple of failures that made her sneeze when her nose hit the milk.

Meredith watched the stubborn little survivor while I washed up and changed out of my beige slacks and dark brown cotton shirt. Everything I wore smelled slightly acidic from working in the darkroom. As I pulled on a pair of grey sweats, I called out from the bathroom, "How are things going with you? Is Leah still headed here for the weekend?" I wondered if she would say anything about the other partner who might be in town this weekend, and how she would find the time to work things out with Leah if this Martin Foster were here.

"I'm really worried about Vernie spilling her guts to Leah. She's been hassling me all week, trying to get me over there before her jackass husband, Bert, arrives. His union election is Friday, and he's coming up Saturday to spend a two-week vacation. Vernie kept going on about how he's planning a working vacation after his victory, and we could probably still slip away somewhere. I finally had to tell her to stop calling. Said I was sorry, but I'd made a mistake. She got real pissed off."

I hated suggesting anything to further confuse the situation, but I said, "But don't you have the same thing over her that she has over you? She certainly can't want Bert to find out."

Meredith shook her head. "She claims the jerk wouldn't care all that much, that she's had other affairs during their marriage, and he knows all about them."

"Well, I hope things work out for you and Leah. And just to give you both plenty of room, I'm going to take off Saturday morning, probably stay overnight somewhere. The place will be all yours. Maybe Veronica is just bluffing."

"Maybe," Meredith said, softly, "and maybe it won't make any difference. I don't expect a hell of a lot, but you might want to be off the property anyway just in case things don't work out and we start yelling at each other again."

Before I could pull the question back, I blurted out, "What is it you two fight about? It's clear you care for Leah. Isn't there some middle ground you both could find?" Almost immediately, I thought, *Now you've gone and done it, Nicholson. So much for your so-called noninvolvement strategy.*

Setting down her mug with a soft thud, Meredith said, "Money, mostly. She doesn't like how I make mine, and I don't like how little she settles for when she's making hers. With her skills she could be making three or four times what she does working for nonprofit organizations." As she shoved the mug away from her, Meredith's eyes turned hard and distant. "What the hell? Maybe I should give Leah a taste of her own medicine. I wonder how she'd like it, coming up here, expecting to see me, and I'm just not here. Why should she think I'm just sitting around waiting for her to show up?"

I almost bit my tongue to keep from saying, " Because that's exactly what you're doing," but I caught myself and said simply, "I see. Well, whatever happens, you'll have all the space you need to work things out."

As she got up to leave, Meredith paused to say, "Thanks for letting me think out loud in here, and thanks for taking on the little one. Don't take off too early Saturday. I'm sure Leah would like to meet you since she seems to enjoy your photography. I promise we'll try to behave until you're gone."

We agreed that I would come by the house for coffee on Saturday morning before I took off, and if the old mother cat had not returned to claim the baby, Meredith would take care of her until I got back. Closing the door behind Meredith, I looked at the hungry kitten and thought, *Way to go, Nicholson. Here's your first chance to take on a responsibility, and you hand it off within forty-eight hours.*

From the angle of the sun's rays through the skylight, and the cozy warmth of the cabin, I knew I had slept late Saturday morning. After one last stretch to loosen my muscles, I slid out of bed and scrubbed myself clean at the tiny basin. No point in taking a shower if I was going to work up a sweat exploring new places today. I vowed to find a motel that offered a tub so I could enjoy a long soak.

I made a half pot of coffee and poured a cup to carry around while I took care of the kitten and prepared for my excursion. There had been no sign of her mother since I last saw her on Wednesday, but the little one seemed to be managing as long as she was fed several times a day. I grabbed a banana from the knobby kelp basket that served as a fruit bowl, and wrapped up the leftover apple bread Meredith had put in my freezer last week. Packing the food plus a thermal container with the rest of the coffee into an open-topped canvas bag, I added my point-and-shoot camera. I wanted to be just another tourist taking snapshots.

I dropped the canvas bag and a small overnighter with a change of clothes in my VW, then scooped up the kitten and a bag with her supplies, including a special orphan kitten milk-replacement formula I'd picked up at the feed store. It was close to noon by the time I crossed the yard from the cabin to the main house. I noticed Meredith's car was not in the carport, but parked next to my van was a boxy, candy-apple red Jeep Cherokee with a sunroof, which I assumed was Leah's. A small windsock made in the colors of the lesbian and gay liberation's rainbow flag fluttered from the antenna.

A whacking sound came from the side of the main house, and

I ambled over to deposit my charge, who was now curled up in the crook of my arm. As I turned the corner, I was surprised to see, not Meredith, but the back of a dark-haired woman, naked from the waist up. A red plaid cotton shirt lay on the ground a few feet from her. Carefully she placed a log on end, tapped in a heavy wedge, and swung high to smack the wedge with the flat end of a sledgehammer. The log split neatly. I waited until she completed her swing, retrieved the split logs, and placed them on the stack next to her.

"Good morning. Is Meredith around?"

The woman turned toward me without any gesture to cover herself or appear modest. She was much younger than Meredith, or me for that matter, and her dark brown hair was short, but full and lively. Her light brown eyes bored into me as she said, "Good question. I got here and found logs and tools laying around like she was getting ready to start a job, but never got to it. Her car is gone, so maybe she remembered an appointment or errand. But she knew I was coming. Then again, maybe she's just paying me back for my not visiting sooner. I expect we'll be arguing about it before long."

With the expectations these women had of each other, it was a wonder they had stayed together as long as they had. Stepping forward to extend my hand, I said, "You must be Leah, I'm..."

With a broad grin, she put down the sledgehammer and took my hand in both of hers. "I know exactly who you are, Ms. Nicholson." Her voice had the mocking tone of an impudent student.

I looked more closely at the full, round face and sturdy form, just a couple of inches shorter than mine. Her face was somehow familiar, and the robustness of her body, which was full and strong, reminded me of something from my past. Like an electric shock, her name came back to me. "Lorie Hillyer? My god, it's been..."

She interrupted me again. "Yes, I know, almost eighteen years." With a wry smile, she gestured at her body. "Honest, I'm not an exhibitionist. I'm not always taking my clothes off, but I was afraid I'd split the seams of my shirt swinging that thing. Plus it's pretty hot work."

Still trying to put it all together, I began to stammer foolishly, "B-but your name...what about...?"

Picking up the sledgehammer, she struck the wedge in another log, turning it into kindling. "That's easy. After the shit my father

gave you for those pictures, and the way he treated my mom, I wanted
no part of his name. They split up before I graduated high school.
Besides, Little Lorie never did feel comfortable to me. When I was in
college, I decided to be my own person, recreate myself. My diploma
still said Lorelei C. Hillyer, but the day after graduation, and ever
since, I've been Leah Claire. Claire's my mom's name."

My head brimming with questions—and with memories—I
sank into a weathered Adirondack chair and watched this woman swing
the heavy tool effortlessly. The logs made a cracking sound as the wedge
was driven deep into the wood, and finally the two halves would fall
away from each other. Leah's smooth, tanned skin glistened in the
dappled sunlight, and stray wood chips would glance off her broad
shoulders or full breasts as they flew up from the strikes. Occasionally
the sound would startle the kitten, and she'd jump or cower deeper
into my lap.

I watched the supple body work for a long time, almost for-
getting that I had planned to leave for the weekend. Finally, gathering
my thoughts, I said, "Meredith told me that collection of my work is
yours. Are you a photographer, too?"

She shook her head. "Nah. But thanks to your class I can do a
reasonable job taking pictures when I need to for my work. You should
see the cutesy shots I took on a zoo job I had, but I just take them to the
drugstore for developing. That's not my thing."

"But you looked for my books?"

She said flatly, "Yes. I wanted to have them."

What I wanted to do was sit here all afternoon and quiz this
woman on her life since high school, her relationship to her parents
now, and whether she had indeed been the one to show my work to Dr.
Huberman. But I knew that at any moment Meredith would return and
there could either be a major argument or a tender reunion. I wasn't
ready to be a witness to either. I picked up my bag and turned to go.
"I'm off to find some walking trails and play tourist for the rest of the
weekend. It's something I haven't taken the time for 'til now, but I've
been advised to do it before the rainy season hits. Meredith said she'd
look after our little friend here until I get back tomorrow, but maybe I
should..."

"No, it's fine. Leave her with me until Meredith decides to
come home." Leah put down her tools, slipped on the plaid shirt that

she left unbuttoned, took the kitten from me, then fell in step beside me as I walked to the van. "She must be a foundling. She's much too little to be away from her mother."

I explained what had happened before opening my car door. She looked at the old van and said, "Say, didn't you have a VW back home when you were teaching? A 'Bug,' wasn't it?"

"Yeah, I did. The gears just feel right to me, but sometimes I wish I had more power. I really like Meredith's car."

Leah broke a twisted grin. "That was one of her better ideas. This house on the other hand...never mind. We'll settle things one way or another this week." She put her hand on my arm as I pulled on the car door. "Have a good drive. I'll look forward to seeing you tomorrow, maybe catch up on old times." Her voice was casual, almost flippant, but her eyes locked onto mine like a laser beam.

Numbly, I said, "Yes, maybe later. Tell Meredith good morning for me."

With a bitter laugh, Leah countered, "If she's off pouting somewhere, she's not doing much to make it a good morning."

Out of habit I drove south toward the college, stopped at the entrance to the old logging haul road, and walked the headlands for a short time. The views were spectacular, but the terrain made it hard to maintain an aerobic walking pace. The road itself ran behind the industrial strip, and I had seen lots of dedicated walkers trekking on the flat unpaved road. But it offered little in the way of scenery to encourage a reluctant walker like me to stick with it.

I continued the short drive to Pudding Creek beach—a tiny spit of sand below the headland the college was on. A condemned trestle that was part of the haul road divided the area next to the creek from the oceanfront beach. Today it was full of people running on the sand to lift intricate kites into the air, and children trying to climb a high dune so they could slide back down on their bellies. Snacking on the things I'd packed, I watched people at play for a while, but I didn't get out of the van. Finally I left, not willing to mingle with crowds today. My head was spinning with memories and coincidences...if that's what they were.

I decided to stop in the next town south, Mendocino, and take a stroll past the shops and offices on Main Street. In contrast to Fort Bragg, which was workingclass, with its constant billow of steam from the mill hovering overhead, and boats plying the harbor at its feet, Mendocino was a playground. Boutiques for everything from clothes and cookware to birdhouses and weather-reading instruments mingled with art galleries displaying paintings, ceramics, sculpture and hand-weavings. At a gourmet takeout place I bought a small round of focaccia bread, a tiny carton of chicken salad and a bottled iced tea.

Beyond Main Street was a state park dedicated to the views and trails found on the headlands. The ocean breaking against craggy cliffs was breathtaking on this bright fall afternoon, but I was still too caught up in my past to enjoy the splendor of the present.

After a while, I abandoned my search for a new walking path and decided to just keep driving. I wanted to test my skill on the nar-row winding route that hugged the edge of cliffs, and offered gorgeous seascapes for those brave or foolish enough to take their eyes from the road. I worried a little about my increasing tendency to be alone, but convinced myself it was just a reaction to breaking up with Gina and trying to figure out where my life was headed after this most recent failure at a relationship.

I had hoped that this respite from my life in Dubuque would give me ample time to consider why I hadn't been able to make a success out of any relationship in the last ten years. But the problems of Pacific Arts College, Meredith and Parisi, Meredith and Vernie, and Meredith and Leah kept intruding. Now Lorie Hillyer, or rather, the woman she had become, was back in my life... at least for the moment.

By around four o'clock I found myself in the town of Point Arena, about forty miles south of Fort Bragg. When I saw the old light-house, I regretted not packing a better camera and good lenses, but took the tour anyway and savored the view unobstructed by the black frame of a viewfinder. The changing light was mesmerizing, and I stayed on the lighthouse grounds to watch the sun melt into the sea. I did take some pictures with the auto-focus camera I had brought, but it was invigorating to be totally caught up in a visual display, without worrying about shutter speed, focal length and light sources. I rel-ished the freedom until it was almost dark, then pampered myself at a pricey inn with an ocean view and a promise of breakfast delivered to the room. An old claw-footed tub provided a leisurely soak, and I sat reading a mystery novel until the water turned cool. I finished the book sitting up in the high, soft bed while munching on the meal I'd picked up in Mendocino.

After sleeping late and indulging in the pampered care of the inn's hosts over breakfast, I was refreshed and prepared to dredge up the past with Leah, if she was still at the house. I thought about slipping back into the jeans and sweatshirt I'd worn during the drive down, but finally dug out a pair of cocoa brown wool slacks and a cream-colored sweater that I had packed to wear only if I decided to do something special. Maybe I needed the dressier, more sophisticated look to restore a bit of the teacher-student distance between myself and Leah. Seeing her yesterday, a full-grown, voluptuous woman, had been a shock. I had not been able to look away as her body glistened with sweat over the stack of logs to be split.

It was afternoon by the time I got back to the house. Leah's red car still stood alone in the carport. As I killed the engine, she appeared on the porch, her solid figure framed in the doorway. She wore a soft, salmon-colored sweater with a high cowl neck. Her dark brown hair shimmered with reflected highlights. "Hello," she waved. "I thought it might be Meredith, and I came out to tear into her for letting me cool my heels here overnight."

I expected her to head back into the house, but she walked toward me, her hands in the pockets of her snug jeans. Gesturing with a tilt of her chin she said, "How did your sight-seeing go?"

"Okay. Actually I started out looking for walking trails. The exercise books say you should have seven—one for each day of the week. Then I decided to just drive down the coast."

Leah moved closer to me. "If there's time, I'll show you one of my favorite spots, Seaside Beach. It's a little bit north of here, but it's great at low tide when the sand is firm and flat." She put her hand on mine. It was warm compared with my icy fingers. "How about a drink?" she nodded toward the house. "I've got a good fire going because it's bound to get cold tonight, and I found a couple of bottles of wine chilling in the fridge."

With a bitter grin, she added, "I suspect Meredith was planning to seduce me into staying the whole week, then got pissed off and decided to 'teach me a lesson about neglect' as she calls my behavior. Some strapping kid came by shortly after you left yesterday. He was disappointed to see me working on the logs. I guess Meredith had hired him to do the job, but he slept late and missed his appointment with her."

I hesitated only briefly before accepting her invitation for a drink. My curiosity about this vision from my past was much stronger than the voice of caution. While Leah uncorked the wine in the kitchen, I sought out the volume of Adrienne Rich poetry and thumbed through it. Leah smiled as she brought the wine in. "This is a nice Chardonnay. I think you'll like it." When she caught sight of the book, she said, "That's one of my favorites, too. *A Wild Patience Has Taken Me This Far*—pretty damn far from the Mississippi shores, I'd say. Back then I thought a jug Chablis was a classy white wine." Sliding into a seat next to me on the couch, she added, "If you'd like to take the book back to your cabin, please do. I doubt I'll be much in the mood for poetry after Meredith and I have it out."

Diving into the entanglement I'd avoided for weeks, I asked, "That sounds pretty final. Are you planning to leave her?"

Sipping her wine thoughtfully, Leah said, "I think I left her a long time ago, and I kept hoping she'd give up trying to hold onto me so I wouldn't actually have to say the words. For all my tough talk, I've been a goddammed coward about it."

Softly I said, "So it wasn't a very pressing job raising funds for homeless zoo animals that kept you away."

Leah shook her head. "The zoo job ended a couple of months ago. I stalled about moving because I knew I couldn't live here with her, then they asked me to help raise money for the Democratic presidential campaign. I don't know if he has a chance or if much will change with a Democrat, but we've got to try something to get that fucking Bush out of office before another Supreme Court justice bites the dust."

I noticed that Leah swore easily, like many of her generation, and a generational gap is what it felt like between us, although there was probably only eleven or twelve years difference in our ages. I wondered if the age difference between Leah and Meredith had been a problem. Ignoring her political comments for the moment, I said, "I'm curious, Leah. What made you decide to come up now, to confront

Meredith at this particular moment?"

"Actually, the confrontation with Meredith is sort of...a by-product. I've gotten involved in the presidential campaign in ways besides fund-raising. I want to get someone from the women's community here to head up a local get-out-the-vote campaign. It'll be a real short-term commitment since the election is a week from Tuesday. A lot of them think no man's worth lifting a finger for, and usually I'd agree. But this is different."

Although I'd only drunk about a third of the wine in my glass, Leah reached over to top it off, taking my hand in hers to steady the glass as she poured. "And I figured that, since I used to live on the Spread, I was the logical one to come up."

"You lived out there?" I was surprised, assuming her objections to Meredith's house meant she didn't care for the area as much as Meredith thought.

"Yes, I moved up here in '84 after I blew off my first job over an asshole superior who wouldn't keep his hands off me. Isaac Winters was still alive, and I was here the whole time his fucking nephews were trying to screw Willow out of her home."

"Then it's not this house or living on the North Coast that's come between you and Meredith."

Leah got up and poked at the fire with a pair of tongs. "Only Meredith comes between me and Meredith. I love it here and would move back in a minute if I thought I could find enough work. Right now it's too expensive to commute from here to other fund-raising assignments. Meredith bought this damned house because she knew I loved the Coast. She thought she was buying me, too."

"If you love this area so much, why did you leave the Spread?"

"Living on the Spread was fun when I was a kid, but despite my best efforts, some of my parents' middle-class values rubbed off. I need a little more security than that, especially now that I'm getting older."

I choked on my wine trying to stifle a laugh. "Older? Lor—Leah, you're what, thirty? Give me a break!"

She looked a little indignant. "I'm thirty-two, and I know that doesn't sound old, but I want to fix it so I can quit working before I'm too old to enjoy it."

"Thirty-two sounds very young to me. And it also sounds like you and Meredith have a lot in common."

With a final jab at the fire, sending sparks flying, Leah put down the tongs and returned to sit next to me again. "Not really. She's found what she thinks is a gold mine of opportunity on the North Coast and is selling it off to the highest bidder, making sure that people like me will never be able to own anything here. Even that job at the college is just another tactic. It doesn't pay shit, but it adds to her reputation as a hot-shot real estate saleswoman."

Leah leaned back on the couch with a sigh. "I'm sorry. I didn't mean to rehearse my next fight with Meredith. I get so angry about what she's doing because it affects average working people and even the women on the Spread, who don't care about owning property. If retail merchandise, and even food and gasoline prices keep soaring because this becomes a resort area, these people will be forced out." Her hand slipped lightly onto my shoulder as she added, "But that's not what I wanted to talk with you about at all."

Her eyes were the color of dark polished amber as she caught my gaze and tried to hold it. But I dropped my eyes. Holding my wine glass between my palms I rolled it back and forth gently, watching the little ripples in the shimmering liquid. "Did you show Dr. Huberman my books?"

Leah sat up straight, moving a little away from me. "Yes. At a party Meredith gave last spring while I was visiting, I overheard him whining about a documentary photo class he wanted to offer this term, but the artist he'd invited backed out for a better offer in Los Angeles. I thought of you and, the next morning before Meredith and I took off on our trip, I brought my copies of your books down to his office. I didn't hear any more about it until Meredith told me she'd rented the cabin to you. Guess he liked your work," she finished, with a self-satisfied grin.

My ego only slightly deflated to know I wasn't his first choice, I asked another question, the one I'd wanted an answer to even longer. "Back in Missouri, at school.... Did you know then that you were a lesbian? And what about the other girl? Cathy, wasn't it?"

"I knew. I wasn't sure what it meant, but I knew. As for Cathy, no. Last I heard, she was married. She was just trying to be my best friend, and all I did was get her and you into a shitload of trouble."

We talked some more about the past, Leah filling me in on

events in our mutual hometown after I left the school to avoid a public fight to keep my job. She had left later to go to college, then never went back to St. Martine to live. At one point Leah excused herself, returning with a platter full of sliced cheese and cucumbers, chunks of skinless poached chicken breast, spicy flat breads and carrot sticks. Without a pause to consider declining, I was sharing a cold supper with her.

I was fascinated by the sound of her throaty, grown-up voice coming from a face I still thought of as a shining adolescent, so I let her go on explaining the kinds of fund-raising she did. Then she asked me about my work. Occasionally my thoughts went to Meredith. She had seemed so excited about having even a small chance with Leah, it was hard to imagine her stomping off in a snit, even though she had toyed with the idea of letting Leah get a taste of the neglect she felt. Actually, I was starting to worry about Meredith, but Leah didn't seem concerned, and she knew Meredith better than I did, so I let it go.

Before I knew it, it was past eleven o'clock. Picking up the book of poetry, I asked, "I would like to borrow this, if I may."

"Of course. Help yourself to anything on 'my shelves,' as Meredith calls them." Leah looked at her watch as we walked to the front door. "Speaking of whom, I wonder where she's spent the last two nights. I thought sure she'd be back to have it out by now."

For the first time a look of remorse clouded her eyes. "I should have been more honest with her this summer. I must have really hurt her. Sometimes I forget she's not always the hard-boiled real estate wheeler-dealer trying to turn a real working town into a glitzy shopping mall."

Leah's reference to Meredith's real estate goals made me wonder again if her absence was of her own making. As we stood by the door, I decided to tell her about the fallen tree and our suspicions about Pete Parisi. "It was clear he was trying to intimidate Meredith and keep her from soliciting property owners in the harbor. Maybe I'm getting worried over nothing, but Meredith has her share of enemies, too. Maybe it's time to contact the police."

After a long, silent moment, Leah said, "I will. First thing in the morning. I don't think they'll do anything unless she's been gone over 48 hours; maybe it's even 72 hours." Softly, she added, "I've never needed to know that kind of information."

With a reassuring squeeze on Leah's arm, I got up and whispered, hopefully, "And probably you won't this time. But it's worth a call in the morning, just to be sure."

Instead of saying good night at her door, Leah walked with me to my cabin, insisting I needed help carrying back the kitten and her paraphernalia. At my door, she handed me the kitten and said, lightly, "If you're free tomorrow, we could take that walk on the beach. Low tide's about two o'clock."

"I'll have to see who stays after class. It ends at noon, but I usually stick around to keep the lab open for a couple of hours. Thank you for this evening, Leah. Good night."

Before I knew what was happening, Leah leaned forward, pressing me against the door of the cabin with her hips. Her lips found mine; her hands held my face. When I stayed perfectly still, not responding, Leah stepped back. "I'm sorry.... No, I'm not. I've wanted to do that for a very long time."

I started to try and explain how she'd caught me off guard, but she had disappeared into the darkness between the cabin and the main house.

With some trepidation I watched as all of the students filed out of my classroom. I wasn't sure I wanted to be free to go walking with Leah. One or two students stopped to explain why they weren't staying to continue working in the darkroom. For some others, it was obviously too beautiful a day to work. The sun had completely burned off the morning fog, and it was a crystal clear, miraculously sunny day on the North Coast. Those not going out to photograph some aspect of their assignments were probably headed for the beach to surf or just soak up the rays. Connie was the only one left when I went back into the darkroom.

She looked up from her locker where she was putting away her photographic paper. "Hi. I was just hanging around to help clean up. It doesn't look like anyone else bothered."

"Thanks," I grinned down at her. "I thought putting up that sign 'Your Mother Doesn't Work Here' would give them the message. I guess I'll have to be a little more direct. I really do hate lecturing so-called adults on responsible behavior."

After testing the photo fix for freshness, Connie helped me pour it into a storage bottle. Since it was the first time we'd been alone since the party over a week ago, she asked, "Did you enjoy the party last weekend?"

"Very much. It's exciting to see women living in a cohesive community like that."

Connie looked away. "Yeah, well let's hope we can keep it together."

"Oh? I thought things were going well out there. What's the problem? Some disagreement among the residents?"

Connie turned on the light in the room. She looked at me, not accusingly, but with a deep question in her eyes. "No. For once we're absolutely united on this. We got a visit at daybreak Friday from the county drug task force. Four guys with two drug-sniffing dogs. They said there was a report we were growing pot on the Spread. They drove all over the property for three hours in a four-wheel drive vehicle, scaring the sheep and even the kids. Doris' little girl had nightmares all weekend."

"That's terrible, Connie. Why would anyone...?" I looked again into her serious eyes and realized why she had stayed after class—to question me. "Connie, you don't think I would do anything like that? I hope you know me better than that by now."

Her gaze dropped slightly. "No, Alix, I don't think it was you. But it could have been Meredith."

"Why would Meredith know or care anything about a little pot?"

Vehemently, she spat, "Because property seized in a drug raid can be confiscated and sold—sometimes even before there's a trial."

Meredith's gluttony for property to sell was undeniable, but she was a woman and a lesbian. I refused to believe she would betray her own to turn a profit. "You're wrong, Connie. At least I hope so."

When Connie didn't answer, I added, "It *was* a phony tip, right? They didn't find anything, did they?"

"No. There wasn't anything to find. We did have a problem with one woman last spring. They had to ask her to move out. The managing council doesn't care how people live. Sometimes there's a little pot at parties or ceremonies, and one or two residents might have a small amount around from time to time. But she was cultivating the stuff among the tomato plants in the greenhouse. It put everyone in jeopardy, and they had to revoke her contract and burn all of her plants, but no one would turn her in. It would have just brought trouble down on all of us."

After locking up the photo lab, I put a hand on Connie's shoulder to get her to look at me again. "Connie, I hope to God you're wrong about Meredith, but if she did try to turn in the women on the Spread to make a buck, I'd move out of the cabin. I wouldn't do anything to help finance someone who would jeopardize women like that. Please believe me."

With a slight nod, Connie said, "I do believe you. I'm sorry I even thought you might know anything about it. I like you a lot, Alix, and it hurt a little to think you might have known and not warned us."

It was only a little after one when I got back to the cabin. There was still no sign of Meredith's silver Explorer in the driveway, but Leah was raking the brown spots out of the lawn like a busy home owner. "Hi," she called. "For a woman who likes land so much, Meredith sure as hell doesn't know how to treat it once it's hers."

Dropping her rake in the grass, Leah wiped her forehead with the sleeve of her grey sweatshirt. "Still up for a walk on the beach? My campaign meeting is tonight, and if Meredith isn't back by the time it's over, I'm outta here tomorrow."

I had some trouble meeting her eyes after last night's surprising kiss. Oddly, I felt like the younger, less sophisticated party, but I attributed that to the uncertainty of Leah's relationship with Meredith and our former ties as student and teacher. Thinking of her as anything different would take some time. I decided it was silly to let one kiss become a major issue, and said, "Sure. Give me a few minutes to change."

Leah grinned, "Make it half an hour. I could use a little cleanup, too. If we leave here about 1:45, we'll hit the beach at pretty close to low tide."

Leah's remark about leaving tomorrow finally sank in, so before turning down the path to my cabin, I asked, "By the way, did you talk to the police yet?"

Leah shrugged. "I called the sheriff's department and the California Highway Patrol. The sheriff's office is understaffed and said there wasn't much they could do unless there was some evidence of foul play. They suggested I give the CHP her license number. Hell, I can't even remember what it is, but I gave them a description of her car. Anyway, it's probably as I suspected. Meredith bailed out on this weekend to slap me in the face."

She started toward the main house, then turned back to me with a smile. "I'm glad you didn't let that little lapse of mine get to you. Like I said, I've wanted to know what that would feel like for years. Now I know." With a flippant wave, she bounced onto the front deck and dashed into the house.

It was too warm for my combat jacket so I topped off my outfit of a black T-shirt, sand-colored cotton slacks and an old pair of running shoes, with a photographer's gadget vest. As I dressed, I wondered if Leah's kiss had been her way of slapping back at Meredith. Despite all the times I'd promised myself to steer clear of their personal relationship, here I was in the thick of it, half-wanting to run and half-wanting to stick around for the possibility of another kiss.

Seaside Beach was something special. Lying below a sheer headland dotted with impressive homes, the beach was wide, and as Leah had promised, the sand was easy to walk on after the surf had scoured it smooth. Rocks twenty to thirty feet high showed signs of marine life deposited during high tides. A stream at the northern edge carried small stones onto the beach and carved a channel to the sea.

I had to shout to be heard above the pounding surf. "You were right. This is a great place."

Leah nodded. "I'm glad you approve." Pointing south, she said, "If we go down this way, we'll meet the Ten Mile River as it makes its way to the ocean. There are lots of little wave caves and crevices for exploring. Come on."

Leah charged ahead of me, her bright red shirt and white cutoffs making a colorful splash against the smooth, empty beach. The twelve years of youth she had on me more than made up for my longer legs. After having seen her half-naked swinging a heavy sledgehammer, I also guessed she did more than aerobic walking as a workout. I stopped to catch my breath, and Leah came back to meet me. I shook my head. "Go on at your own pace. I'm enjoying this very much. We can climb around the caves together once I get to the other end."

She took off again, her strong legs striding right up to the edge of the surf. Occasionally she bent down to examine a shell or stone. Leah knew the beach well, and obviously wanted to stretch her legs. I continued to amble behind, taking in the sights and sounds of what Connie had once called "living on the edge." I compared that with the safety I knew living in the middle, back home in Iowa. Always in the middle—of either substitute teaching assignments or photo shoots; always in the middle in relationships; never letting myself fall in love or commit all the way.

I patted the pockets of my vest and realized that, for once, I'd come away without any camera equipment. Freed in a way, not having to be careful of sand or water damage, I started walking closer to the surf, almost playing tag with the foamy waves as they broke on the sand.

Just ahead, I spotted another formation comprised of three rocks, the largest being pointed. Through the rock I caught a glimpse of blue sky, and wondered if this was what Leah had referred to as a wave cave, created by eons of crashing surf. I jogged easily on the level sand and reached the formation. Clambering over a circle of small rocks, I stepped inside the cave to inspect the inner walls and see what treasures they held.

And then it happened.... My foot slipped off the still damp edge of the opening. Surprisingly, it landed on something soft and mushy. Since my eyes had not quite adjusted to the dim light, at first I thought it might be a bunch of seaweed or an article of clothing abandoned long ago. It was neither. "Oh, my God, this can't be," I gasped out loud. It was a ghastly sight. There, next to my foot, lay the ashen, bloated face of what was once Meredith Coates.

She was dressed in khaki slacks and a pale green sleeveless top, and I could see with a growing sense of horror that her skin had been scraped raw. Her arms and legs showed signs of being attacked by the teeth and claws of small creatures. A string of kelp was partially wrapped around her body, its bulbous end lying almost like a little pillow next to her cheek. I swallowed hard, then opened my mouth to scream, but no sound came out. My heart was pounding, I felt light-headed and wondered if I was going to pass out. Gritting my teeth, I rested my head on the cool rock and swore silently. *No, dammit, Nicholson. Not this time. Stay on your goddammed feet.*

Before I could raise my head, or scream, or get out of the cave, Leah was peeking in the opening, with a grin on her face. "Interesting, aren't—"

I took a deep breath and thought fast. The least I could do was spare Leah the horrifying sight I had just seen. With all my strength, I lunged out of the cave and pushed her away from the opening.

Grabbing her, I shouted, "No, don't come in here! You don't want to see this. It's Meredith...she's...d-dead..." And then, in a softer tone, I added, " It's too late for us to help her. We've got to call the police."

I wrapped an arm around Leah and looked into her suddenly pale, stunned face. Clearly, she was having a hard time grasping what I had told her. As I guided her back to the Jeep, she stumbled along beside me, dazed, saying nothing.

The voice of the sheriff's investigator droned in the background as he spoke on the phone. We heard him requesting that various investigative teams be activated. Their orders were to find out all the circumstances surrounding Meredith's death—where, when, and how she died. Leah and I sat quietly on the sun porch, her fingers entwined in mine. She had not cried or screamed or even talked much since my discovery of Meredith's body, but every time I tried to let go to do anything, her hands reached for mine, gripping them tightly, refusing to let me out of her sight.

When the deputy, a tall, slender man about forty named Jerry Gossett returned to us, he asked softly, "Ms. Claire, I know this is a bad time, but I really do need to speak with you alone. So if Ms. ah..."

"Nicholson," I finished for him. "Alix Nicholson. I'm teaching at Pacific Arts this term. Ms. Claire and I are...old friends from St. Martine, Missouri."

"Thank you, ma'am. If Ms. Nicholson will excuse us for a few minutes, we could go into the sitting room."

Leah looked at me fearfully. Her face seemed younger and even more vulnerable than the way I remembered her, sitting in the principal's office, trying to explain away nude pictures she and her friend had taken of each other.

I nodded encouragement and let go of her hands. "I'll be right here, Leah. Just tell him what you know." I turned from Leah to the deputy. "I assume you'll want to talk with me, too, since I was the first one to see the bod—see Meredith. Plus, I may know someone who might have wanted to do her harm."

The deputy touched the brim of his hat like a TV cowboy might to show deference. "Thanks again, ma'am. You're right about that—and any information you have would be most appreciated."

Although Leah and the deputy were in the next room, the open construction of the house made it easy to hear his questions and her answers. Patiently, Leah explained that she had not seen Meredith for over two months, and although they called each other regularly, they had been catching only their answering machines recently and had not spoken for more than a week. Leah knew only a little about Meredith's real estate deals, explaining frankly that usually Meredith's reports led to fights about her tactics.

The investigator led her through the events of the past days, starting with her arrival on Saturday, through our awful discovery an hour ago. Gossett's voice was a soft, persistent monotone, but Leah's was barely audible, her words hesitant, often slightly slurred as if she were still in shock. My heart went out to her.

After a few more questions about Meredith's family (apparently there were no siblings and both parents were dead), her daily routines (which Leah knew very little about since she had not lived here with Meredith), and her will, (if one existed. Leah said she knew nothing of it.) Finally, the deputy thanked Leah and said he was through, for the time being.

Leah, her eyes glassy and unfocused, stepped onto the sun porch just briefly. "Alix, I'm going to go lie down for a while. After the deputy is done with you, please don't go back to the cabin. Don't leave me alone in the house just yet."

I promised to check in on her after Gossett left, then turned toward him, awaiting his questions.

"Ms. Nicholson, when was the last time you saw the deceased?"

"Around five o'clock Thursday. We were taking care of this little one." I pointed at the orange kitten. "Its mother had disappeared."

Gossett jotted down the information as if committing anything to paper was a chore. I wondered if, as a child, he had clenched his tongue between his teeth when writing as I had seen so many young students do. He checked another page of his notebook. "That mother cat wasn't by any chance one of them black and tan and white ones, was it?"

"Why, yes. How do you know—? Have you seen one like that?" The officer sort of peeked up at me through darkly hooded eyes.

"It was found under Ms. Coates's body."

"The cat? Dear God, why would anyone hurt a cat that didn't even belong to Meredith?"

Gossett sighed deeply, his face once more bland, impassive. I got the impression he had let on about finding the cat to get a reading on my response. Apparently, even I was a potential suspect.

"Hard to say, ma'am. Now, you didn't see her or hear anything unusual on Saturday morning?"

"No. At home I live in the city, and I've learned to sleep through a lot of noises. In fact, I had trouble my first few nights here because of the quiet."

"Yes, ma'am," he said, making more notes. "Ms. Nicholson, what were you doing on the beach today?"

"Just walking. Leah promised to show me Seaside Beach before she went back to San Francisco. I had told her I needed some compelling reason to get out and get my exercise. Back in Iowa, I sometimes ride my bike to work, but I'm not brave enough to try it on that narrow, winding highway." I grinned, trying to relax myself as much as put him at ease.

Deputy Gossett nodded, but didn't return my smile. "I see. It was Ms. Claire's idea to go to the beach. Was it also her idea for you to climb into that cave? You know, ma'am, that's a dangerous spot. Even at low tide folks get themselves trapped by sleeper waves comin' in. Maybe that's even what happened to Ms. Coates."

"Are you saying you think she died accidentally?"

"Could be. But she's been living up here a little while. Ought to know better than to get caught out there at the wrong time."

Could Meredith have tried to hide out there, maybe sulking about Leah's indifference, and just got tossed around by the surf? If that was the case, why wasn't her truck still there? I had never quite bought Leah's theory about Meredith's motives for disappearing, despite Meredith's own words the last time I saw her. Now I was convinced she had not left this house voluntarily, or possibly even alive.

"Deputy Gossett, you might want to go talk to a shop owner down in Noyo Harbor, Pete Parisi."

The deputy looked surprised. "I know Pete. You're not thinkin' he had anything to do with this?"

"All I'm saying is that he was very angry about some of Ms.

Coates's sales down in the harbor. He accused her of trying to destroy the fishing village.... And he threatened her if she continued pressing the zoning commission to establish an historic village in the harbor."

The deputy looked down at his shoes. "Ma'am, everyone knows Pete's got a bad temper, but he ain't never done anyone no harm."

I remembered the look on his face when Meredith challenged him the first day I was here. "Maybe so, Deputy Gossett, but he did confront her no more than a month ago and tried to warn her away from the harbor. I also think he was following her to work. I've seen his truck and his dog in the college parking lot, parked very near Meredith's Explorer. And it's been in that turnout on the highway about a quarter of a mile from this house several times in the last few weeks. Maybe he was coming up here to spy on her."

Gossett covered his face with his hand as if scratching the stubble of his beard, but I suspected he was hiding a scornful grin about my conclusions.

"A quarter mile, ma'am? Pete's got a bum leg left over from a old boating accident. Fell into the drink watching for submerged rocks when he was coming back into the harbor after a fishing trip. He got tore up good by an outboard driven by some fool drunk tryin' to pass in the narrows." Shaking his head, the deputy added, "No way he could hoof it 500 yards through these woods on that leg."

Frustrated by the deputy's answer for every one of my theories about Parisi, I got up and stared out the window with my back to him. It was nearly five o'clock and the light was fading rapidly, but I kept my back to Gossett to hide my rising anger. I wasn't ready to eliminate Parisi as a suspect, even if the deputy was. Maybe he didn't stalk Meredith from a quarter of a mile away. Maybe he was just hoping to intimidate her by his presence near the house. And when she didn't scare, he...what?

I didn't have it all put together, but Parisi had to be involved. Who else? With a jolt, I remembered my conversation with Connie earlier today, but pushed it back down. Surely no one on the Spread could have been so enraged by the phony drug tip and subsequent raid that they would come after Meredith!

Thinking of the Spread reminded me of Meredith's story about her brief affair with Veronica Battles. I turned to face Gossett again, "Deputy, you might want to speak with Mrs. Battles. She lives across the road, and she may know a little about Meredith's whereabouts recently. You might even want to ask where she was on Saturday morning." I stopped short of revealing Meredith's indiscretion with Veronica, I guess to protect Leah. Even though she had been prepared to leave her, I didn't think Leah needed to know that Meredith had been unfaithful just yet.

The deputy's left eyebrow raised just slightly, but he said nothing as he made more notes on the narrow spiral pad. He studied them for a moment, then said, "That's all for now, ma'am. I may have some more questions for you later, after I get some reports back about the time of death. Right now, all we know is she was missing 'bout two-and-a-half days, and, at some point, took a nasty crack on her head."

He started to leave, then turned back to me. "By the way...if the medical examiner's preliminary report indicates foul play, I'll be comin' back out here to look around the house, search for clues that might lead us somewhere. Should have his report later this evening. Sooner we get on it, more likely we'll find what we need. I could get a warrant, but if Ms. Claire is willing..." He eyed me cautiously, as if hoping for a protest or excuse, but I refused to play his game.

With a naivete I came to regret, I said, "I'll tell Leah about it and have her give you a call. I don't think a warrant will be necessary, but please wait until you hear from her before you send anyone out."

He tipped his hat again. "I'll be waiting, ma'am." He dug a business card out of his well-worn wallet, the wallet and card both curved by the hours Gossett sat on his back pocket. "I hope Ms. Claire is feeling better soon. I know it musta been a shock."

I double-locked the door behind the deputy, not really concerned that Leah or I had anything to fear from Meredith's murderer, but more to create a barrier between us and the brutal reality the deputy represented. The light was now completely gone, replaced by another layer of fog—this one carrying a fine mist that created lacy rivulets on the tall windows of the sun porch.

In the kitchen, I hunted for the fixings for a pot of coffee, and thought of how my stepmother, Ellen, had always tried to mend the world's problems by sitting down with a cup of coffee. I rarely acknowledged that any of her habits had stuck to me. She had married my father and come into our home and made it hers just as I was reaching my rebellious teen years. Suddenly I regretted how I had made all of our lives hard for a while, until I discovered the magic inside my camera.

The whir of the bean grinder broke the deadly silence in the house, and I worried about disturbing Leah. While the coffee brewed, I went to check on her, realizing with amazement that I had never been on the second floor of Meredith's house. The large main bedroom was empty, although the bed looked like it had been slept in. The red plaid shirt Leah had more or less worn the first time I saw her Saturday was tossed onto an upholstered blue armchair with other presumably dirty clothes. On a wide window seat was an open suitcase. I thought how sad it was that Leah had stayed in this room as if it were a one-night motel stop, and wondered if she would have given the same impression to Meredith if she had lived to spend the weekend with Leah.

I left the bedroom and opened another door. Behind it was a smaller room with a medium-sized desk holding a laptop computer. Leah was lying on a rust-colored, folded-up futon, her face toward the back. The futon rested on an armless frame that was much too short for Leah. I started to back out of the room and closed the door.

In a soft, muffled voice, Leah said, "Don't go, Alix. I wasn't asleep."

"Couldn't rest in the bedroom?" I asked as I pulled up the desk chair to sit next to her.

Leah shook her head and sat up stiffly. "No. I thought I was pretty much over Meredith before I came up here, but, God, this hurts like hell."

I put a hand on her shoulder, and whispered, "Of course it does. You can't expect not to feel anything just because you had decided you couldn't be her lover anymore. She was a human being, a woman, a compelling presence, regardless of her business schemes."

Leah was silent for a moment, then reached up to take my hand which still rested on her shoulder for support. "This isn't how I wanted to renew our acquaintance, Alix. There was so much I've been wanting to say to you, but now..." She let go of me, dropped her head into both her hands and rubbed her face. Still there were no tears, just pain and exhaustion in her eyes.

"Look, Leah, the deputy wanted to send a team out to search the house. We were supposed to call and let him know if it was okay.

I'll tell him you're not up to it tonight."

"No, it's alright. I'd rather get it over with. But could you also call Willow, tell her what's happened and cancel the meeting out at the Spread?"

"Of course. Do you have her number handy?"

"It's ah..." Leah stopped to think. "I can't remember it off-hand, but I'm sure it's still listed. The phone book is downstairs next to the kitchen phone."

Leah and I stood up together and she followed me out of the room. As I continued down to the kitchen, I could hear Leah moving around in the main bedroom and upstairs bath.

When I got Willow Shade on the phone, she listened quietly as I explained what had transpired. Her voice quavered with rage when she finally spoke. "Meredith dead at Seaside Beach? Is there no safe and sacred place left for any woman?" With a sigh, she thanked me for the call and said she would check in on Leah in the next few days. Then I called the sheriff's office and left the message for Deputy Gossett that he could send his men out.

I was still sitting at the counter on a tall stool near the phone when Leah came down the stairs in a fresh pale blue oxford shirt and dark grey slacks that showed only the slightest creases from her suitcase. She got two cups out of the cupboard over the sink and poured coffee for both of us. She gave one cup a slight nudge across the kitchen counter toward me and, with a thin smile, said, "As I recall, you take your coffee black."

"And you seem to remember a whole lot about me for someone who only spent a semester in my class."

Leah shrugged and pulled a stool up to the counter so she could sit across from me. "I guess you came into my life at what they call 'an impressionable time.' I found out everything I could about you." She peered at me over the rim of her cup as she sipped.

We talked of inconsequential things that did nothing to erase for me the sight of Meredith's lifeless, grotesquely bloated body wedged among the rocks, on the floor of the wave cave. I still wasn't sure how much Leah had seen before I'd pushed her away from the entrance.

Finally, Leah got up, saying, "I suppose I need to call the campaign office and let them know I won't be back for a while." Speaking as if in a trance, she added, "I wonder how long it will be before the police release the body. It's funny, yesterday Meredith had a name, and I was so angry about the 'game' I thought she was playing with me, that I used that name frequently and profanely. Now all I can manage to call her is 'the body.' "

I walked around the kitchen counter to stand next to her. Slipping my arm around her waist like a big sister, I said, "It's just your protective mechanism at work. It won't hurt so much if somehow, who she was, can be separated from what's left."

"I suppose. Thanks for everything." She turned and wrapped her arms around my neck. Her body trembled slightly, but there were still no tears. I pulled her close and held her for what seemed like a very long time, neither one of us willing to let go.

Finally, Leah's arms loosened slightly, and I moved away, murmuring, "I haven't done anything yet."

"Perhaps I wanted to thank you before I ask you to do something else."

"Name it."

Leah paced the few feet from one side of the kitchen to the other, holding her clenched hands close to her chest, and nibbled her thumbnail with her front teeth. "When the search team gets here, could you sort of show them around? They're welcome to take anything of hers or mine that they think might help. I just don't think I can handle being here while they paw through stuff."

"I'll take care of it. Where do you want to go?" I was worried about letting Leah drive anywhere in her state. One minute she seemed fine, barely affected by Meredith's death, the next she was vague, moving and speaking as if in a daze.

"That's the rest of the favor. I don't want to be too far away in case they do have questions. Like I said, I want to get this thing over fast. Could I hang out in your cabin...just while they're here?"

"Of course."

Leah smiled gratefully and went upstairs. She had some phone calls to make.

Within the hour three men in a county car drove up and parked next to the house. They were followed by Deputy Gossett driving alone in an unmarked vehicle. I met them on the front porch.

"Evenin', ma'am," Gossett said with his slow drawl. "Is Ms. Claire around?"

I hesitated, hoping Leah would not be disturbed, then knew this was not the time to start lying to the cops—besides, both of our cars were in plain sight. "She'll be resting in my cabin while your men conduct their search."

"Well, I need to talk with her. It won't take no time at all. I just got a couple of questions. My boys can get started in the main house." Turning from me, he yelled to his team, "Bobby, you take the inside of the house. Jack, you and Fred see if you can find anything around outside or in that tool shed." Without another word to me, Gossett headed for the cabin behind the house.

Neither Leah nor I had foreseen the possibility that the search team would split up. I'm not sure why I pictured the investigators trailing after Gossett or some other team leader from room to room like hounds on a scent. I guess the events of the day had done nothing to promote clear thinking.

I was torn between following Gossett to steady Leah while he questioned her and keeping my promise to her to stay with the police search team. And which part of the team should I try and keep up with? I decided anything found by the pair of officers outside or in the shed would be pretty straightforward. If there were any questions, it would probably have to do with things inside the house.

I followed the officer Gossett had called Bobby through the

sun porch into the main house. "If there's anything I can help you with, please let me know."

"Thank you, ma'am." His tone was as polite as Gossett's, but his manner was more formal than the folksy drawl of his boss.

It felt a little frivolous under the circumstances, but I was getting annoyed by these men in their thirties and forties calling me "ma'am" like I was...what?...some old-maid schoolteacher. With a wince, I realized they weren't far off the mark.

"Bobby," who didn't feel the need to further introduce himself, poked into cabinets and drawers in the kitchen, ran his hands above and behind books on the shelves in the sitting room and bent down to look under pieces of furniture. He even turned back the sitting room rug that had a small wrinkle in one corner. When he was satisfied there was nothing sinister on the floor beneath it, he replaced the rug, smoothing it down carefully.

I followed him upstairs, where he first inspected the guest room/study. He looked around for a moment, then asked, "Is there a cardboard box or carton around here somewhere?"

I shook my head. "I haven't spent much time in Meredith's house, but I don't recall seeing anything like that."

With a shrug, he opened one of the desk drawers and neatly stacked the contents on the futon, then proceeded to fill the drawer with files from the filing cabinet—pending sales, petitions to governing boards, requests for environmental impact statements—anything that might provide the police with the name of someone with a motive to harm Meredith. Before leaving the room, he picked up and confiscated one last file marked "Personal Finances—MJC & LSC."

In the bedroom I noticed Leah had picked up the dirty clothes I had seen earlier and the bed covers had been straightened up a bit. Leah's maroon canvas suitcase was now closed and standing next to the window seat.

The officer sorted through the clothes hanging in Meredith's closet, stirring up a conglomeration of scents. A soapy, freshly laundered fragrance from the clean shirts and blouses mingled with Meredith's bracing, almost manly cologne; the faint but earthy aroma of a woman's body came from sweaters and jackets she'd worn a couple of times. My eyes stung with the realization that the things in her closet now seemed more alive than the woman they had belonged to.

Breaking into my thoughts, Bobby asked, pointing to the suit-case, "Is this yours, ma'am?"

"No, I'm staying in the cabin out back. I believe that's Leah's—Ms. Claire's suitcase. She was up here to see Ms. Coates."

Hesitating just a moment, the officer said, "I'd like to take a look in it. I'll have to go ask the lady's permission unless you can tell me if she was part-owner of this place." He started to leave the room.

"Look, Officer, I'm sorry I only heard Deputy Gossett call you by your first name..."

"Siebert, ma'am."

"Officer Siebert, I don't know what Ms. Claire's arrangement was with Ms. Coates regarding the house. I'm sure it's all there in those papers you have. I wish you wouldn't disturb Ms. Claire. She's taking this very hard. She and Ms. Coates were...quite close. At least until recently. She asked me to take care of anything having to do with this part of the investigation. She said you could have anything of Ms. Coates, or hers, if it would help find out what happened to Ms. Coates."

The officer paused briefly, and I was beginning to think he would go off to find Leah and verify that before proceeding any further. Then, in a single motion, he grasped the large, soft-sided suit-case and swung it onto the window seat. He felt around the main section carefully, barely disturbing the shirts and lingerie neatly folded on top of a pair of wool slacks in a muted blue-green plaid and some jeans. He pulled the zipper on her cosmetics case and poked around with one finger and was about to close the luggage when he remem-bered to check the long pocket across the top inside. His hand disap-peared and came back out with the red plaid shirt which had been rolled into a ball and stuffed in the pocket. He shook out the garment and felt the cuffs and body of the shirt, then stopped. Taking a side-long look at me, he folded the shirt, placed it in a plastic evidence bag and dropped it into the drawer he had used to collect files and papers from Meredith's office.

After a cursory look in the two bathrooms, Officer Siebert picked up the drawer and met the rest of the team outside where they were standing in the dark behind their police cruiser. Nodding in my direction, Siebert said, "We'll see that all of this gets back to Ms. Claire...when we're done with it."

Deputy Gossett's car was gone from the driveway. The two

police officers who had searched outside loaded the trunk of the car with two plastic bags. Officer Siebert transferred the items he had collected into a cardboard file box with a lid and handed the drawer to me. "If you would, ma'am..." Drawing me closer with just a touch on my arm, he added, "And ma'am, I'd appreciate it if you'd verify what we've got here."

"Verify?"

"It's procedure, ma'am. Sometimes people accuse us of not returning things we never had in the first place. Fred, show her the list."

Standing next to their open trunk, I went through the things with Officer Siebert: the files from Meredith's study, a few articles of clothing, the sledgehammer and wedge Leah had been using the first morning I saw her, a couple of shovelfuls of dirt and wood chips from the area around the wood pile, and two pairs of work gloves. With a nod, I confirmed that the list matched the items and watched the officers drive away.

The night was cold and starless as I picked my way out to the cabin to tell Leah the police were gone. I shuddered at the realization that twice in eighteen months I'd found myself confronted with sudden, violent death. My heart still ached when I thought of of my last brush with death in D.C. I mourned the violent killing of daring, impulsive Sandra, and thought how much the world had lost with her murder. What kind of turn had my luck taken for me to be thrown into two such predicaments? As a photographer, I'd made some perilous journeys, put myself into uncomfortable situations with the homeless, a fledgling street gang and other dicey conditions. But now I was seeing a cruel side of fate that I had never had to acknowledge before.

10

"They found Meredith's car," Leah said softly as I entered the cabin after watching the search team drive off. "That's what Gossett wanted to tell me."

"Did he say where?"

"That's the weird thing. It was nowhere near Seaside Beach. It was driven off the road at the south end of Fort Bragg, just above Noyo. They towed it to the sheriff's substation and his men will go over it in the morning." After a long silence, she added, almost in a whisper, "And they'll be looking at everything. They won't be positive until the medical examiner does an autopsy tomorrow, but they *are* treating it as a murder."

The mention of finding Meredith's car near the Noyo Fishing Village immediately brought my thoughts back to Pete Parisi, but maybe that's what the killer wanted the police to think. Parisi had been pretty vocal in his opposition to development at County Supervisors' meetings and planning hearings. If it had been Parisi, wouldn't he have abandoned the car far away from his stamping grounds, just as he had the body? But what if that was part of his plan to take the heat off of himself? He knew there was a witness to his threatening Meredith, and he.... I stopped myself. This was all too confusing.

I flopped down next to Leah on the love seat and soaked up the warmth of the fire she had started in the wood stove. *Let the cops handle it, Nicholson.* At first, this case had seemed fairly obvious, but Meredith had stepped on a lot of toes lately. I could envision half a dozen different scenarios, and at some level, they all seemed plausible—from Parisi creeping up on Meredith while she was setting out tools for the wood cutter who showed up late, to Huberman panicking about the future of Pacific Arts College. And even the seemingly gentle Willow was not above suspicion. Despite her quiet bearing, there was a passion in her that could have exploded when the haven she had built was threatened.

No, sorting out the truth in this death would be far from simple. The only thing I wanted to do about this murder was talk to some of the women on the Spread—to convince myself they had nothing to do with it. That way I wouldn't feel guilty not telling the police about their suspicions surrounding the drug raid. I leaned back and listened for a while to the Vivaldi that Leah had put on the portable CD player. It seemed a very long time ago that Meredith had loaned it to me along with some other discs.

I put my hand on Leah's arm and rubbed it lightly. "How're you doing?"

"A little better. At least I think I can manage to go back to the house without needing a constant attendant. Thanks for letting me hang onto you that way. I was a fucking basket case this afternoon."

I wanted to tell her not to be so hard on herself, but stopped for a couple of reasons. Maybe she needed to act tough to get through the next few days, and maybe I felt like I was already in too deep. Although I had known the girl who sat in my art class almost twenty years ago, I had only met the woman the day before yesterday. For all I knew, she could have killed Meredith in a fit of rage, and merely played the role of worried lover for my benefit. Leah had kissed me last night to satisfy a childish fantasy, or because she was angry with Meredith, and today she had come close to flirting with me even after we got back from the beach. I had assumed her behavior meant she was in denial about Meredith's death, that the full weight of that fact had not penetrated her thinking. What if the truth was that she simply didn't care? Either way, I saw caution flags every time I closed my eyes.

But when I looked at Leah's crumpled form, which seemed somehow smaller than before my awful discovery, I couldn't believe she had a murderous streak in her. Or perhaps I just didn't want to face that possibility. Without asking if she wanted it or needed it, I got up and started dinner for the two of us. When events in the real world got too hard to follow, remembering the directions in my favorite recipes helped center me. I laughingly called it my mealtime meditations, but the uncomplicated process of taking things one step at a time really did clear my head. But it was late, and I was fighting exhaustion, so I kept the meal simple.

Setting a pot of water on the range to boil, I minced a couple of garlic cloves and sautéd them in a mixture of half butter, half olive oil, then tossed in some matchstick cuts of zucchini to stir-fry while the fettuccine was cooking. I tossed the fettuccine with the zucchini-garlic mixture and set it on the table with some grated cheese. I didn't have a decent dinner bread to round out the meal, so I settled for serving whole wheat toast.

When Leah noticed what I was up to, she left the cabin saying she would be right back. She returned with a bottle of white zinfandel, tasty but not remarkable. With a wry grin, she said, "No point in wasting the good stuff. I doubt if either of us could tell this wine from the pasta water tonight. Maybe sometime before I go back to the city, I can pick up a bottle of really good wine to grace some other dinner table of yours."

We nodded across the table as if making a pact to meet again under happier circumstances and ate in silence. There seemed to be nothing left to say about a day filled with such turbulence and tragedy, yet to speak of anything else seemed disrespectful. I wanted to ask Leah some questions, any question that would absolutely convince me of her innocence, but I couldn't think of any way to begin.

After the meal, Leah tried to help clear the table and start the dishes, but I took her hands in mine one last time. "No, let them be. I'll take care of them later. You should try and get some rest. Sooner or later the police will be here either to talk to you again or tell you they've found the killer. You need to be ready for them. And when it's all over, you'll need to make some decisions about Meredith. I can't believe she expected to die anytime soon and left instructions or anything. Whatever happens, you're going to need all the strength you can muster."

Leaning her head against the door jamb, Leah cursed softly under her breath. "Oh, damn. You're right. How the fuck will I know if I'm doing the right thing, doing what she would have wanted?"

Tilting her face up to mine to look into her eyes, I said, "Just do the best you can. It really won't make any difference to Meredith now. I'll help any way you want. I've got photo labs and classes tomorrow and Thursday. Do you want me to take some time off until the cops are through poking around?"

Pulling her head up, Leah took a deep breath and squared her shoulders. "Thanks, but, no. I've got to get it together. What the hell? I was about to lose her anyway, because that was my choice. I just don't get why this is so fucking hard?"

I didn't say anything because she knew the answer as well as I did. Leah might have decided she couldn't live with Meredith and her get-rich schemes, but no one deserved to die that way, violently and alone, at the hands of a deadly assailant.

With a brief hug for support, I let go of Leah and watched her head back to the main house. While getting ready for bed, I tried to come up with a plan to talk with Connie tomorrow and to get her to help me talk to others on the Spread.

After a mostly sleepless night, I decided there was no point lying in bed any longer trying to get back to sleep. My head was still filled with questions and doubts, and my heart was heavy. At five a.m. I gave up and got out of bed, washed the dishes from last night's supper, and after a shower and breakfast for myself and the kitten, I left the cabin with an extra pair of shoes and socks. I had decided to walk for a while on Pudding Creek Beach, which was likely to be deserted this early in the morning. It was nearly two hours until my nine o'clock class, and I wanted to try to get some photographs that didn't look like everyone's clichéd seascapes.

The ocean was remarkably calm, and the river flowing gently into the sea seemed to be just a ribbon stretching down from the same smooth surface. A pair of white herons picked at morsels on the river banks and several ducks bobbled in the still water. I was beginning to understand the allure the ocean along this coast had for people, especially women like Willow and Connie—and Leah. Standing alone in the sheltered coves and bays, listening to the ocean's perpetual lapping against the shore was like exploring an immense womb. The headlands all around offered protection from the turbulent sea rushing in, and wading into the surf could be as perilous as birth itself, as dangerous as trying to live in this world.

I picked my way along the sand, skirting long trunks of driftwood and branches blown off the pine trees above the beach, the soft sand making the walk a real workout. After about forty-five minutes of slogging through the uneven terrain, stopping only to frame a shot from time to time, I was winded and ready to drive around to the top of the headland, get into my classroom and prepare for the day to come.

Striking a more direct route back to the van, I watched for rocks and fragments of driftwood in my path. I was about thirty feet from the van when I looked up to see Pete Parisi standing directly in front of the driver's door. His battered white pickup was pulled crosswise over the narrow dirt road, obstructing any escape in the van— almost the same tactic he had used to block Meredith getting into her house the day I first saw him. The yellow Labrador retriever sat in the truck bed, panting amiably.

"Pretty, ain't it?" he snarled, pointing toward the ocean with a thick length of driftwood. "Won't be long before you'll have to pay to walk on that beach. And you know what you'll see? Oil rigs. Even if any fish make it back into the ocean from the rivers they've wrecked up north, they'll be poisoned by the crap that comes spillin' out of them monsters."

Rather than confront him directly, I decided to follow the thread of his conversation as I continued toward my vehicle. "It doesn't have to be that way, Mr. Parisi. People can still tell the government how they want their land to be. Maybe working together, they can be heard."

"Yeah, right. Just like they listened when they closed down the commercial fishing so a few rich guys could torment some poor coho salmon into a boat and feel like tough guys."

"But the sport fishermen bring money into the area, too, don't they?"

"Sure, for minimum-wage jobs at fast-food restaurants and discount stores. Hell, I can't compete with their prices for tackle and camping gear."

I was just over an arm's length away from him when I finally said, "Look, Mr. Parisi, I've got to get to my class. They'll be expecting me soon."

A twisted grin broke on his face. "Nice try, lady. Classes don't start for another half-hour. Lots can happen in that amount of time."

He moved just a few inches closer to me, raising the chunk of wood almost menacingly, then dropping it back onto his shoulder. I backed away.

"A little nervous, are ya? Well, ya oughta be. It ain't nice spreading gossip to the cops, slanderin' folks. I didn't have nothin' to do with that broad croakin', but maybe now she's not around to promise everyone the moon, some of them folks'll come to their senses."

I couldn't decide if Parisi was a real threat, or if he was toying with me. The wrong decision could cost me a lot. Parisi was just my height, and if Gossett was right about his crippled leg, I could easily outrun him. It would be my only chance if he did get violent, because even if I managed to overpower him temporarily, my van was stuck until his truck was out of the way. And what about the dog? Labs were generally easygoing, but if his master ordered it, would I have to outrun a four-legged beast, too?

I was mulling all these options, poised on the balls of my feet, ready to bolt as soon as Parisi dropped his guard for an instant. Suddenly, from the side road above the beach, I heard my name.

"Hey, Alix, can you come open up the darkroom? I was hoping to get started a little early this morning." Connie's casual wave from a hundred yards away felt like arms opening wide to welcome me. I heard myself breathe again.

Jogging lightly, Connie came down to join us on the dirt road. She even gave the dog a little scratch as she passed Parisi's truck. "Good morning, Alix. Hi, Pete. Hope I didn't interrupt anything."

Parisi nodded a gruff hello to Connie, then turned toward his pickup with a final word to me. "Just remember what I said, lady. It ain't nice talkin' about folks you don't know, makin' accusations."

As we watched Parisi drive off, Connie asked, "What was that all about? Pete sure looked pissed off."

I told Connie about my first encounter with Parisi when he threatened Meredith, and how I had passed the information on to Gossett, who seemed to dismiss the idea.

Connie nodded. "I heard about Meredith on the radio this morning. How awful. I know it looks bad for Pete after that stunt, but I'd have to agree with the deputy in general. Pete's got a big and sometimes foul mouth, but I've never heard of him getting in any real trouble. He was assigned to my floor after his accident. He cussed a lot about the jerk who drove the other boat, but it never amounted to anything. I think mostly he's scared because things are changing so fast."

Trying not to sound as if I was dismissing Connie's opinion, I said carefully, "Whatever his problem, thanks for breaking it up. I think I could have handled Pete, but I wasn't sure the dog was much of a friend. Come on, I'll give you a ride up to the college, and we can get the darkroom set up."

"Thanks," Connie said as she climbed into the van. "How's Leah taking this? She hadn't seen Meredith for some time, I'd heard. And now to come up and find her dead..." Connie shuddered slightly, but didn't finish her thought.

"She's okay, I guess. I don't really know her all that well. We only met on Sunday." Somehow it seemed too complicated right now to explain my past connection to Leah, who was then Lorie.

In the photo darkroom, Connie helped me set up two trays each of paper developer, stop bath and fix, then I turned out the room light and flipped on the safelight, which started out a very faint orange and got considerably brighter as it warmed up.

Back in the classroom, Connie laid out a couple of sleeves of negatives on the light table and examined them with a magnifying loupe. After a moment, she called me over. "Take a look at these two, she said, pointing. "Which one do you think is sharper?"

I examined the negatives she had indicated. "I think they're about the same in sharpness, but Number 24 seems to have a higher contrast. You probably need to do test strips on both of them to decide which one you'll like better."

Connie made a face. "That's what I was afraid of. I was trying to save paper by picking one or the other. I'm really enjoying this class, but, it's getting damned expensive."

"Tell me about it. I've been doing this for twenty-five years, and I don't think I've broken even yet. But maybe I can help. I managed to get one of the manufacturers to give the college a small supply of paper in lieu of a grant. It's an off-brand, but I've tried it and the results are comparable to other brands, but the surface is a little different." I opened my locker and handed her a sealed package of photo paper. "I think you left early the day I announced that this stuff was available. I sort of hated to make a general announcement about it, because of one student I won't name who seems to be shooting baby pictures commercially and using the school's facilities, but it is intended for everyone's use."

Connie smiled and wrinkled her nose. "You mean Tony O'Keefe. Yeah, I've seen some of his stuff floating around in the wash tank. I don't think he likes kids all that much." She looked at the package, and said, "Thanks. I'll put it to good use."

"I know you will. I've seen your work so far, and it's good. Keep it up." I hesitated a moment, not wanting to offend Connie into thinking I was trying to buy her help. "Look, Connie. I need a favor, but if you're uncomfortable with it, we'll forget it. I'll figure out another way."

"What's the problem?"

"I know you care very much for the women out at the Spread, and I was moved by their spirit the one time I was out there. I haven't told Gossett that some of them suspected Meredith of planting a phony tip about drugs on the land. I don't want to cause them any trouble, if there's no need."

Connie looked at me gravely, but without rancor. "You're not saying you think any one of them could have killed Meredith? Alix, those are gentle, spiritual women on the Spread."

"All of them, Connie? Are you absolutely sure? Someone ended a woman's life, and I pray to whatever goddess guides any of us, that the someone was not another woman. I don't want to involve the deputy unless there's a reason to investigate further, but I won't be comfortable not telling him until I've convinced myself that no one out there had a motive for murder."

Connie thought about it for a minute. "Would you have to do it like a real interrogation?"

"I'll do it whatever way you want me to. They don't have to know I'm trying to eliminate suspects. I just need to get to know them a little better for my own peace of mind."

Picking up her negatives, Connie headed for the darkroom, but before she closed the door, she said, "Okay, I'll help you, but just to show you how wrong you are about them."

C onnie agreed to invite me out to the ranch the next day, Wednesday, ostensibly to take photographs of women living in an alternative community for a possible documentary series. It made me sad to use my craft to essentially spy on these women because the idea of such a series was a good one. Of course if I were to do it, I would need to live among them for a time to make it authentic. But if I ever told Gossett about the group's anger at Meredith, no one on the Spread would trust me enough to let me do a photographic series on their lives.

I stayed with some students working in the darkroom for a couple of hours after class, but the previous sleepless night and my encounter with Parisi had worn me out. I needed to get back to the cabin to check on Leah and relax a bit, and so I left Connie to close up when the last student was done.

Leah was sitting on the sparse lawn which was mostly brown from six years of drought in Northern California. Despite the condition of the grass, Leah was carefully plucking weeds as far as her arms could reach. As she flung weeds into a heap, bits of soil fell onto her bare legs and into the cuffs of her black shorts. I wanted to sit down next to her and see how she was doing, but the unspoken dress code for teachers at Pacific Arts was a bit more formal than the casual and eclectic dress of most coastal residents. I was afraid of getting grass stains on my light grey wool slacks—the best pair of pants I'd brought with me to California. I said a brief hello before heading for the cabin to change, but I felt a tug of emotion that I knew would draw me back into her presence very soon.

As I stepped out of my black loafers and stripped off the slacks and a navy blue button-down shirt, I wondered if the dress code was attributable to Dr. Huberman's rather unbending personality. As the head of the art department, he kept himself separate from me and, as far as I could tell, most of the other members of the department. Only the potters and painters got away with wearing casual, "unprofessional" garb, as he called jeans and pullover shirts.

Although it was late afternoon, it was still sunny enough for short sleeves. After a final fling of my bra, I slipped on a loose-fitting lavender T-shirt. From the window, I saw Leah sitting in the grass, still picking at the weeds that were the primary source of green left in the lawn. Something told me she probably needed to talk, but when I put on an old pair of sneakers to join her in the yard, I reluctantly admitted to myself that I was the one who needed to be close to her. With a nonchalance I didn't really feel, I pretended to be walking around the spacious yard to stretch my legs and ended up standing above Leah, who was still stabbing at the ground.

Gesturing at the weed pile Leah had made, I asked, "Does that really help at this time of the year?"

Leah nodded. "It helps some if you get the roots out before the rains come, if they ever come again. Mostly it helps me." She brandished a small, straight tool with a V-shaped point. "I haven't figured out who's getting the most pokes with this: the fucking bastard who killed Meredith, Gossett for his inane questions, or Meredith for putting herself in such danger with her greed."

"Is that all it was? Simple greed?"

Lowering her chin almost to her chest, Leah murmured, "No, not really." Raising her voice a little, she continued, "With Meredith it wasn't so much greed as it was pathology. Look, what I told Gossett about Meredith's family; it's not quite true. Her father is still alive somewhere, but Meredith swore she'd die before she ever let him near her again. Now that she's dead, I'll try and honor that vow by keeping him absolutely out of this."

"She was abused as a child?" My heart ached for the child who escaped brutality only to end up dying violently.

"Pummeled is more like it. She said it was never sexual, just plain beating."

"Did her father have a drinking problem?"

"Her father had a control problem. He couldn't control her with words or with the promise of money, so he did it with his fists. She got out of that house before she was seventeen and never looked back. She was trying to make so much money that she would never have to go back to him for help, and being successful was the way she disproved her father's predictions that she'd amount to nothing. I even think one of the reasons she bought this house was to finally prove she had a real home." Choking back a sob, Leah added, "Once, she told me that all she needed to make it complete was me."

Leah had stopped jabbing the ground and sat very still. With a fierce determination in her eyes, she fought to regain her composure. I got up and touched her shoulder. "Come on, it's getting chilly. Why don't we go inside? I'll practice my fire-building skills." Leah took the hand I offered to help her up, and we walked back to the main house, her hand still in mine.

As I crumpled up some newspaper and broke twigs over it in the fireplace, I asked, "Were you just reminiscing, or did something happen today?"

Leah leaned forward, her elbows resting on her bare knees, her fingers gripping her short, but unruly hair. "Gossett was here. He confirmed that Meredith didn't have an accident in the wave cave. She died from a brain hemorrhage following a blow to the back of her head, *before* she was moved to the cave. I don't know if he was being evasive or suspicious of me or what, but he claimed they haven't come to any conclusions about whether she was actually struck by some kind of weapon, or if she hit her head on something." She sighed deeply, then added, "He also said the medical examiner would probably release the body by the weekend."

"I never did buy that theory about Meredith getting caught by a sleeper wave while out on a walk." Squatting down in front of her, I circled her wrists with my hands to look into her eyes. "Leah, I'm not sure you want to hear this right now, but I think Meredith would not have left here on her own to spite you. The last time we talked she was excited about your coming up, a little scared, too, but certainly not vengeful. She was willing to do whatever she could to keep you. I have a gut feeling the evidence is going to show that she was killed right here, with me sleeping less than a hundred yards away."

For the first time, at least in my presence, Leah's eyes welled up with tears. "Damn, I don't want to do this," she blurted out, unsuccessfully choking back her sobs. She clenched both fists and brought them close to the sides of her head, then her hands opened and she covered her face with them.

I let her vent her grief and anger while I continued to work on the fire. With the sun almost gone the room was cool. I found a tan and rose lap robe on the armchair and draped it lightly over Leah's shoulders. I held her arms for a moment to let her know comfort was here if she needed it, but she was lost in her anguish and barely acknowledged my touch.

I pulled the armchair a little closer to the fireplace and settled in for the evening to keep the flames going until Leah could take care of herself again. I began to consider how I would conduct interviews with the women on the Spread without raising suspicion.

Connie had explained the working of the Spread on our way out there on Wednesday morning. There were eight permanent adult residents, plus Connie, who stayed with Doris and her six-year-old daughter, Doe, on weekends or other times she didn't have to get to work early. Two other women had young children, and a lesbian couple from Southern California had built a spacious cottage on land rented from Willow. One of them was a rather famous film star, and they welcomed the safety and freedom of the Spread. Since they didn't live there full-time and couldn't contribute to the work of keeping it going, they sent a substantial sum twice a year at property-tax time.

By three in the afternoon, with Connie's help, I had photographed and talked to five women, and we were now headed toward Doris's cabin.

"Connie, we don't have to do this. I'd be happy to take Doris's picture sometime with you and her daughter, but I don't think I need to question her."

Connie shook her head. "What's fair for one is fair for all. The only difference is that I have told Doris what you're after. I won't keep secrets from her."

"You're smart, Connie. You and Doris seem to have something special, and you're right not to jeopardize it." It made me glad to know that some lesbians knew how to hold onto and nurture love. And I wondered if I'd ever figure out how to do that.

Inside the cabin, Doe came running to greet Connie, who picked her up and draped her around her neck like a feather boa. "Okay, Baby, let's go for a spin." Stepping back into the yard, Connie held the child firmly as she spun around several times in a tight circle, the little girl squealing with delight.

Doris, a heavy woman barely five feet tall with soft brown curls, was wearing a long, multicolored caftan that swished softly as she followed her energetic child. She smiled at the antics of the two loves in her life. Quietly she said, "I have spinal arthritis, and she got too big for me to play with her like that a couple of years ago. Sometimes I think Doe believes Connie stays around just for her." Turning her eyes back to me, she added, "Connie told me what you're doing. It made me mad at first that you could think any of us would harm any woman. But then I realized you could have just told Gossett we were angry with Meredith and let him come out here and nose around. I don't care if he is the law, he's a man, and men just bring violent auras wherever they are."

I felt awkward. "Doris, I told Connie I didn't need to question you. We didn't talk very long the other night, but I don't think you'd risk losing Doe and your own freedom by killing someone."

Doris nodded in appreciation, but it was clear that I was an outsider who had hurt her by wrongly suspecting her friends, and the warm, welcoming smile she had given me the night of the potluck was gone, I hoped only temporarily. But I doubted I would be on the coast long enough to truly regain her respect. I took shots of Connie and Doe's horseplay and of Doe picking naked ladies, lily-shaped flowers that spring up only after their foliage has died down. The long-stemmed pink flowers were almost as tall as the tiny, animated girl.

When the child dashed off to chase her small, wiry dog, I snapped a few pictures of Doris and Connie. The obvious love that showed in the gaze they exchanged brought tears to my eyes. I wouldn't know until I developed and printed this work, but more and more I wanted to really do a documentary project about the Spread, not just pretend to be doing one.

As I photographed, we talked about Meredith and her possible motives for planting a phony tip about drug cultivation on the

Spread. I became thoroughly convinced that Doris could not lift a finger to hurt anyone unless Doe's life was in danger.

Leaving Doris's cabin, Connie said, "That only leaves Casey and Willow. Erin, the only other one you haven't talked to, was in Portland for two weeks and only got back yesterday morning."

I had almost forgotten about the tall, gentle-eyed woman who made this place possible. "Let's leave Willow for last. I'm beginning to think this whole notion of mine was stupid. Of course no one here would be capable of killing a woman in cold blood."

Casey Watson was a short but powerfully built woman of about thirty-five. If my eyes were ice-blue, hers were blue steel. As Connie and I drew closer, Casey gestured angrily, "You can put that thing away. I'm not posin' for no pictures to make people think we're some kinda freaks."

I started to respond, but Connie touched my arm. "Whatever you say, Casey. Can we come in anyway? No pictures, I promise."

Casey's cabin was minuscule compared with Doris's two-and-a- half room place, and even compared to my small one-room cabin on Meredith's land. A single bed took up almost half of the space. A tiny sink was placed in a counter that also held a propane camp stove. A small steel wok sat on one burner. The room held the faintly sweet smell of marijuana recently smoked. Connie looked at Casey sharply, and, as if reading her mind, Casey blurted out, "Ah, don't look so worried, kid. Just a joint I brought back from the city. There ain't no more around here. I'm not stupid enough to keep a stash after that fucking traitor of a broad turned us in. Still can't believe she did that."

"Then you *do* think Meredith Coates was the one who fed the phony story to the police?" I asked, wondering if this woman's rage could have led to murder.

"Who else had a reason? She coulda got this place for a fraction what it's worth if we'd been busted for growing dope on the land."

"You don't think anyone else finds this community a threat?"

For the first time, Casey looked at me without glaring. Instead her eyelids narrowed and her look was thoughtful, probing. "Well, I guess some folks find us pretty weird, but I still think Meredith had the best motive, and she was here just the week before." Suddenly, I realized that the gruff voice and shoddy grammar had disappeared. I briefly wondered if Casey was hiding something other than pot.

She looked at me suspiciously, "In fact, weren't you with her that night?"

Although my appearance with Meredith had been in no way a date, I found myself blushing slightly at the questioning look from Casey Watson. "I'm staying in her cabin this semester. I teach at the college." I hoped that I hadn't sounded as defensive as I felt. I turned to Connie and nodded toward the door as a sign we should leave. But before we went out, I said softly, "By the way, Casey, you're not freaks; pioneers is more like it. Thanks for your time anyway."

As we walked toward the main house which Willow shared with the two women other than Doris who had children, Connie said, "I guess she could have done it. She flies into a rage in a flash, and she was angry enough about the raid. Plus she does sometimes keep a little stash."

"Maybe," I said, thoughtfully. "It certainly seems she would be strong enough to move Meredith's body if she *had* killed her."

Connie and I walked through the main house looking for Willow. Both the inside and outside of the main house needed paint, but it was still easy to imagine the former splendor of the old homestead with its ornately carved fireplace and high-beamed ceilings. Willow was in the kitchen garden behind the house, her back straight as she squatted next to a plot, pulling carrots. She wore a pale blue, open-necked shirt, white painters' pants and garden clogs with thick wooden soles. After selecting every other frilled top in one row, she carefully covered the remaining vegetables with a straw mulch and patted it down. She stood up more easily than my knees would have let me move and acknowledged our presence with a short nod. Stopping at a shelf mounted on the back of the house, Willow laid out her produce and began brushing dirt off each orange root.

Rather self-consciously, I raised my camera and asked, quietly, "May I?"

Willow smiled at me indulgently. "If ya think this is worth capturing, I won't stop ya, but it's just my work. I thought ya said ya were an artist."

"No more than you are, Willow. There's an art to living, and I suspect I could learn a lot from you."

"Alix," Connie said, "if you don't need me anymore for the photo shoot, I really should get going. I'm on the midnight shift at the hospital this week, and I need to get some sleep before I go in."

I thanked Connie for all her help and told her I'd see her in class.

Willow watched Connie head across the field to Doris's cabin, then turned back to me. "Are we going to keep up this nonsense about a photo shoot, or are you finally goin' to get around to askin' me if I killed Meredith? Why not? It wouldn't be the first time someone thought I was a murderer."

This time my blush was deep and hot. I respected this woman for surviving attacks against her character and for the life she had made for herself and for other women, and it hurt to feel like a fool in front of her. I lowered the camera, saying, "I'm sorry," and started to leave.

Her hand like a vise on my upper arm stopped me. "Sit down," she said quietly, but firmly, indicating a bentwood rocking chair next to the back deck. She let go of me, and I complied. She settled in a similar chair a few feet in front of me, her soft grey eyes waiting for me to break the silence.

I tried to explain how this stupid idea had seemed reasonable just yesterday. "I-uh, that is, when Deputy Gossett questioned me about Meredith, I didn't tell him that people out here suspected her of trying to get them jailed or at least thrown off the land. Later, I felt guilty not telling him, but if telling him had caused another invasion of this property, I would have felt even worse. It all sounds absurd when I say it out loud, but I just had to meet as many of the women as possible."

"And?"

"And, now that I have, Deputy Gossett will never hear that story from me." I returned her steady gaze with a resolute look of my own.

A slightly bitter smile played on her lips, deepening the creases around her mouth. "So we've all been exonerated by the self-appointed sleuth?"

I shifted uncomfortably in the chair and said, "I can't exonerate anyone, but I also can't imagine any of you, with one possible exception, would harm another woman."

This time Willow's smile was full and warm. "Then you've met Casey. Don't fall for that mean and stupid routine of hers. It's the way she keeps everyone far away."

"Then she's not—"

"Mean? Sometimes, but the one she hurts the most with that act is herself. Uneducated? Not for a minute. Casey was six months from completing a doctorate in American literature when she was raped by her dissertation advisor. It was strictly her word against his. Guess who they believed? She left the program, found her way here, and now tries to talk like a high school dropout. But she can't always pull it off." Willow said nothing for a moment; her eyes seemed far away, deep in thought.

I wondered how many other stories I'd missed trying to capture these women on film. The Spread deserved to be left in peace, not overrun with men serving the same kind of laws that had failed them already.

"I am sorry, Willow, sorry I ever considered anyone out here a threat to Meredith."

With a sigh, she said, "Nothin' to be sorry for. You don't really know any of us. I was just thinkin', I suppose it's possible Casey could have done it. She was here on Friday, the night before Meredith disappeared. Then, suddenly, Saturday morning she took off for the city. I didn't even see her. She just left a note about switching cleanup chores with Doris for the weekend."

I shook my head. "It doesn't matter. I want to see Meredith's killer in custody, but I won't be the one to point the law in this direction. You were right, I don't know any of you well enough—certainly not enough to put this place in jeopardy."

Willow's smile was sad, but grateful. "I'll be the one to call Gossett if I find out someone here got mad enough to kill Meredith. She was always her own worst enemy. I could tell the first time Leah brought her out here. She looked at this land like a kid in a candy store."

"You sound sad, Willow, as if you've lost a friend."

"I did. She was the best friend she knew how to be, even if that wasn't much. I tried to warn her that she was headed for trouble, but she took my remarks about her practices like they were a joke. I'll miss her."

We sat together in silence for a few moments, each of us lost in our own recollections of Meredith. Mine were few, but they were vivid. It was not hard to understand how Leah had allowed herself to overlook the differences she and Meredith had for so long.

Finally, Willow asked, "Has Leah heard anything from the police about when they might release Meredith's body?"

"Probably by the weekend. She's really concerned about doing the 'right thing' for Meredith, and she's not so sure she knows what that is."

Willow stood up, took my hand and turned me toward a hill in the distance. It was thickly wooded, but a narrow path led to the summit. "There's a place up there we call the Sanctuary. Old Mr. Winters scattered his daughter's ashes there, and after he died I added his to the land." Her face solemn, but serene, she promised, "I'll talk to Leah and see if she'd like to use that spot. I'd also like to have a small ceremony, not really a funeral or memorial service, just a few words to lift her spirit from the violence that ended this life, and wish it peace the next time it finds a home." Willow's eyes flashed in anger as she added, "Plus, the place her body was found needs to be cleansed. Where the sea meets the land is a sacred place on this earth, and her tranquility has been shattered."

I tried to hide my surprise at the metaphysical ideas coming from this woman who seemed so grounded in the land. Even as I thought that, I recognized the natural harmony of honoring the land that provided so much bounty to all living things. "I think Leah would like that very much. I'm afraid I haven't been too much help to her."

Willow took my arm again, but this time her touch was gentle, caressing. "I'm sure Leah's found you to be a comfort right now. You know, she spoke of you often when she lived here. She didn't have much money then, but she made it a point to get that third book of yours the minute it came out."

My mind was reeling with information overload. One moment Willow is revealing her mystical nature, the next she's suggesting that Leah's obsession with me had endured for almost two decades. I rose to leave and Willow followed. Reaching to hug me, she said simply, "Blessed be, Alix. You've been called here for a reason."

On Sunday afternoon—ironically, November 1, the Day of the Dead—just a week and a day after Meredith disappeared, Leah and I drove north to the Spread. A surprisingly small wooden box rested between us on the grey upholstered seat of Leah's red Cherokee. We didn't have much to say to each other. Leah had been tied up with cremation arrangements and estate matters. Apparently Meredith had been the savvy businesswoman right up to the hilt: a recently executed will left everything to Leah, excluding any pending contracts or accounts, which were to be assigned in full to a business partner, Martin Foster, in Sacramento.

Leah had travelled to Sacramento on Friday, the day after a two-inch story had appeared in the local weekly paper reporting Meredith's "mysterious" death, to meet Foster, but she had not revealed anything about the encounter. On Saturday, she had driven off alone late in the morning and returned an hour later with the box that now separated us.

As we passed Seaside Beach, which was nearly deserted due to the dull, overcast sky, I caught a glimpse of a small memorial erected just beyond the parking area. At first it looked like a simple wreath of eucalyptus leaves and wild flowers, but the bottom extended down to form a women's symbol. Inside the circle of the wreath, three calla lilies reached up with their delicate white throats. I wanted to stop, but I wasn't sure Leah, who was navigating the sharp curve with her eyes riveted on the road, had even seen the monument.

At the Spread, Connie, Doris and Willow waited for us behind the gate. When they saw our car approach, Willow, who was wearing a cream-colored robe that reached almost to the ground, with a red sash at the waist, pulled the latch and swung the gate wide to let us in. Leah took the box off the seat, got out of the car, and walked unhesitatingly toward a ceremonial altar about fifty feet from the house. The women formed an honor guard on either side of Leah to escort Meredith to her rest. I trailed a few feet behind. The weathered structure was a primal granite sculpture, about one-and-a-half times life-size, of a full-busted, full-bellied woman, her arms raised toward the sky, her mouth curving in a broad, welcoming smile. At her feet, an oil lamp burned giving off a cinnamon aroma. It was surrounded by a wide circle of colorful, flat stones holding an array of unlit candles. A basket of red apples, purple cabbage and red and yellow peppers rested near the front edge of the circle.

Leah placed the box in the center of the circle and, with a lighted twig, ignited the first candle, moving as if she knew exactly what to do. I suddenly realized that of course she did. Leah had lived here when Winters died, and for all I knew, other residents had passed away on the land as well. She had walked straight to the shrine, and the wonder was that I had not noticed the statue on either of my two previous visits to the Spread. I was the so-called artist; I was supposed to see as much as there was to see and capture it in my lens. Again, I was filled with an awareness that it was time to put the viewfinder down for a while and open my eyes.

I stood back like a visitor at a church service not of her own denomination, and watched the other women one by one light candles and murmur simple blessings to Meredith's spirit. When Connie, the last to light a candle, was done, she handed a glowing twig to me. "Go ahead, the more blessings, the sooner she'll be free to ascend."

Awkwardly, I knelt at the altar and lit a blue candle with the twig. I groped for an appropriate word and finally remembered a line from a May Sarton poem entitled "A Hard Death." I recited the words which had always moved me: "'We cannot save...but we can stand/ Before each presence with gentle heart and hand.' May you be born into gentle hands in your next passage, good woman."

Willow reached over the circle of flames and retrieved the box and basket, offering them to Leah, but Leah's hands stayed at her sides and she shook her head. "No, Willow. I said good-bye to Meredith too long ago. Will you do it please? I don't want to go to the Sanctuary and have to say good-bye again."

Cradling the box in one arm, Willow touched Leah's cheek with her hand and wiped away a tear. Gently, she said, "I'll take her and place her ashes beneath the old madrone tree. The red color of the wood is much like the reddish highlights we once saw in Meredith's hair." Wrapping an arm around Leah's shoulder, Willow asked, "You will stay for the rest of the ceremony, won't you?"

"I'll stay," Leah whispered, leaning over to kiss Willow's softly lined cheek.

Willow and the other two women ascended the steep hill west of the main house softly singing a chant about earth, air, fire and water. Leah and I went to sit on a small stone bench a few feet from the altar. "You could have gone with them, Alix. I'm alright."

With a sigh, I confessed, "Actually, I'm feeling out of my element here, like I might do or say something to offend. I respect what these women believe even if I can't grasp it all right now."

Studying her clasped hands, Leah said thoughtfully, "It's actually pretty simple. There's profound reverence for all life forces: human, animal, plant, and for the earth that sustains them. The earth is treated as a living being, too, one that can be wounded by what is done to her or on her. And it's about living consciously, feeling what you feel and trying to know how your actions can wound or heal other living beings."

"Willow said there was more to the ceremony."

"Well, the farewell is complete, but now that her spirit is free to travel in peace, Willow will bless the place she was found, to cleanse it of the violence that occurred there."

Pulling my khaki jacket tighter around me, I shivered slightly, but I doubted it had anything to do with the cool air. I thought of the incredibly beautiful expanse of sand and sea that my eyes had feasted on before my grim discovery. I wondered if any ritual could erase the ghastly memories or the grisly reality of what had happened there.

As we waited for Willow and the other women to return, Casey Watson came to stand for a moment by the shrine. She was met by another woman. They each lit a candle, then came to join us. The other woman, a tall, deeply freckled redhead, was introduced as Erin Reilly, who had been away at the time of the drug raid and Meredith's murder.

I was surprised to see Casey at all after her tirade against

Meredith, but the occasion seemed too solemn to question anyone's reverence. As if she had tuned into my thoughts Casey said, "I still don't know what to think about Meredith Coates, but violence must be cast out. Where water and land meet is a hallowed place."

By the time Willow, Doris and Connie returned, the light was nearly gone. We went to the altar again and knelt or sat around it. Erin and Casey had placed two bowls in the circle: one was filled with fine, pale sand and the other had clear but briny smelling water. Some of the women took a twig or small stone or leaf from the ground within the circle and dropped it into one or the other of the bowls. Connie touched Doris's hair, snipped off a single curl with a small pair of scissors she pulled from a pouch she carried on her shoulder and placed it in the sand bowl. She whispered, "Doris, you're the most blessed thing in my life."

Leah reached into her pocket and pulled out a purple ribbon I had seen hanging on the wall with a spare key. Again, I was the last to join the ritual, and casting my eyes around, I found a tiny whisker and some orange hairs on the lapel of my jacket from the kitten curled up in the cabin. Remembering how the sight of the mother and baby had touched Meredith, I dropped them into the sand bowl.

Willow picked up the sand bowl and, raising it above her head with both hands, said, "These are the offerings of women who love you, Mother Earth. Use this to purify the place of violence and death." She returned the bowl to the circle and gestured toward a platter of food. In the firelight we ate a simple meal of dark bread, cheese, apples and red grapes. Then, standing up, Willow asked for each of us to take the candle she had lit earlier and follow her.

As we walked toward a small, new-looking building, Leah said softly, "The sand and water were brought from the beach where you found Meredith. Tomorrow Willow will take the amulet she created with our offerings back to the shore and ask for another blessing. When the police find out where Meredith died, perhaps we'll have another ritual."

When we reached the structure, I discovered it was just a deck with five walls but no roof. After climbing the stairs, I saw a large wooden hot tub on the deck, and a stack of thick towels on a bench against one wall. We set our candles on shelves that were hung on each wall.

Willow was the first to untie her sash, drop her robe, and slip into the water, but the others followed quickly. I had been right about the power of Casey's compact, muscular body. Connie and Doris helped each other undress slowly, their eyes locked together, but their hands discreetly touched only the clothes they wore. Once they were in the tub, they linked arms tightly. Erin's body was lean, with soft, almost orange curls between her legs.

Only Leah and I remained to join the women. Self-consciously, as if I had never disrobed for a woman, I dropped my jacket slowly, unbuttoned my blue-and-white striped shirt and slipped off my sneakers before opening the zipper on my jeans. Almost deliberately, I avoided looking at Leah's body until she was in the water. I stepped on the booster at the edge of the tub and threw my leg over the rim to take a place next to her. The water was warm in contrast to the chilly evening, and someone had started a vessel of spicy incense burning. It was a sweet, sensual way to end a difficult day. As a group, we sang in hushed tones everything from Native American chants to Heather Bishop's "Our Silence" and Cris Williamson's "The Changer and the Changed" to, incredibly, "Amazing Grace." At some point during the singing, the wind picked up, lashing tree branches and threatening the glow from our candles.

It was only a little after eight p.m but it felt much later as we drove back to the house. Leah opened the car window despite the strong wind and breathed deeply. "It's going to rain like hell tonight. I hope I brought in enough firewood. I hate using the electric heater and jacking up the gas company's profits." She looked at me with a questioning smile. "You still look confused by it all, Alix."

"Maybe enchanted is more like it. It was a sublime sensation, but I'm not sure what the last part had to do with spirituality."

"It had to do with cleansing. The tub ceremony was mostly for you because you saw a monstrous sight. Perhaps the next time you walk Seaside Beach you'll be able to summon the memory of tonight instead of last week."

"But Willow never said..."

"Would you have been able to embrace all the sensations you experienced tonight if you had known the reason?"

"Maybe not," I conceded.

Finally, we were home. As Leah parked in the driveway, we

realized that the outdoor lights, which usually came on automatically at dusk, hadn't turned on. "I was afraid of that," Leah said. "I thought our neighbors were in bed awfully damn early. There haven't been any lights on for the last mile or so. And it'll be hours before the fucking power company gets it together."

Before I could stop myself, I said, "Come stay in my cabin. I think that love seat pulls out into a bed. The wood stove will heat up the whole room. Much easier for you than trying to get that big house warmed up."

Without answering directly, Leah pulled out a flashlight from under her car seat and got out. The fierce winds pulled at my jacket and knocked Leah into her car door. With a grin, she linked her arm in mine and led the way to the cabin with the steady beam. Once we were inside, I tossed some twigs and paper into the wood stove and got it started before I took off my jacket. I checked on the kitten, gave her some formula-moistened kibble and returned to the fire. We stood together in front of the stove trying to warm our hands, and listened to small branches and twigs coming down on the roof and deck.

Leah touched my shoulder to turn me toward her. Her words caught in her throat as she said, "Do you want to know the real reason I couldn't go to the Sanctuary?"

I nodded, but didn't speak. I wasn't sure I could with her eyes glittering like bits of polished topaz piercing my soul.

"I couldn't take Meredith to her rest because she wasn't in my heart anymore. My every thought was of you. I've tried to dismiss my feelings for you as a teenage crush, but if they ever were that, they have changed as much as I have." Words were tumbling from her lips in a rush, but the sounds were thick with emotion. "Back in Missouri, I made Cathy work with me on those pictures to get your attention, then when everyone got in so much trouble, I was sure you hated me. I think I even got involved with Meredith initially because she was older, a blue-eyed blonde. God, that sounds awful. Later, I did love her for herself, until I brought her up here to share the beauty I'd known, and all she saw was a real estate gold mine waiting to be tapped."

She slipped her arms around me, and whispered, "You didn't hate me, did you? I hated myself for so long because I'd hurt you."

"I never hated you," I said, my voice husky with emotion as I pulled her close to press my lips into her silky, dark hair. The firelight warmed the planes of her face, and I wanted to cover every inch of it with kisses. I let go just long enough to tend the flames even though I knew we would not need it for the heat.

I longed to uncover her body bit by bit—to savor the curves and hollows I had seen only briefly before she descended into the tub back at the Spread. But the air was still cold even close to the stove, so we hurried to undress and got under the covers. Hungrily we reached for each other and clung together as if our lives depended on it. My heart was pounding against her full, supple breasts, and Leah's breath on my cheek was hot and wonderful. With the agility of youth, she rose up over my body and settled hers on top; deftly fitting her nipples against mine, she rubbed our breasts together, licked the underside of my jaw and buried her face in the hollow of my neck. In a strangled sob, she said, "I feel like I've waited all my life for this moment, Alix. My exquisite, untouchable Ms. Nicholson. I never thought this dream could ever come true."

I put my hands on her buttocks and pressed her pubic area firmly against my own. As she rocked above me gently, my vulva filled, even as I felt her sweet juices flow onto my skin.

I thought my heart would burst from pleasure and delight as she slid her body down toward my knees, stopping long enough to suck each nipple and allowing her head to rest in my cleavage for a long moment. When her tongue slipped inside me and found the knot of flesh that ached for her touch, I let out a sound, almost a scream. A sound I'd never heard from my own throat. I closed my eyes and let the sweet untamed passion of this woman consume me.

The annoying beep of my wristwatch alarm broke into a miraculous dream of being loved by a young, lithe and ravenous creature. Reaching for the watch to stop the sound, I arched my back and, to my surprise, felt the warmth of Leah's body curled next to mine. I smiled at the realization that what I thought was a dream was instead a revisiting of last night's pleasure. I luxuriated in the warmth of her body next to mine, and recalled our night together. After hours of passionate lovemaking, I'd been exhausted, and yet I'd found an insatiable desire to return the gift. My hands had lingered over the warm, graceful curves of her body, and my lips had found sweet morsels of skin to caress, and luscious dewdrops of sweat and the juices of love to savor. I slipped my fingers past her vulva and stroked the moist knot of flesh until she lay gasping in my arms. Finally, I had savored the joy of holding her tight while I brought her to a final release. Then we had exchanged a dozen or more kisses, each meant to be a sweet, final good-night kiss. I couldn't remember who had fallen asleep first.

Snatching a glance at Leah as I slipped out of bed, I was startled at how young she looked in sleep. *She is young, Nicholson. Face it,* I thought, as I grabbed a robe and towel and headed for the outdoor shower. Thirty-two didn't seem that different from forty-four on other people, but she had been a high school kid the first time I knew her. And last night! She had made love like a woman possessed, touching me in ways that had exhilarated and drained me at the same time.

The steam generated by the hot water mingling with the chilly morning air rose off my body and mimicked the fog I felt in my head. Loving Leah would be incredible and impossible. Countless things divided us besides age and the miles between our homes. If she got up before I headed off to school, we would have to be clear with each other. Last night was extraordinary because it was so tempestuous and because it could not happen again. Well, I thought, maybe it isn't such a good idea to hurt her, then take off for class. But we would definitely have to talk about it this evening.

When I turned off the shower, the steam cleared, restoring my vision, and I saw Leah, wearing only a long T-shirt, standing just outside the shower's range, smiling impishly as she watched me towel off.

"And where do you think you're going?" she said with a seductive purr.

"Hey, artists-in-residence don't get paid for staying at their residence on class days," I said as I tugged at my robe to get it off the steel hook next to the shower and onto my body as quickly as possible. Although the sight of Leah was warming me up fast, it wouldn't be long before the cool air chilled my naked body.

"Well, unless the school has a collection of propane-powered photo equipment, you might want to go up to the house and call to see if your classroom is even in working order. That shower works on gravity and propane; the fact that its working is no clue that the power's back on."

She was right. The skylight let in so much brightness, I hadn't tried any switches or started coffee. I barely had time to finish getting into my robe before Leah reached for me. She slid her hands under the robe and, with the flat of her hands against my back, pulled me tight against her. "Why don't you go down and call the school to find out if you need to get dressed. This power outage may turn out to be damn lucky for us, again."

I grabbed her shoulders and pushed her away from my body just enough so I could look in her eyes. "Leah, about last night..."

She looked at me warily. "That's the name of some goddammed movie about het sex, isn't it?"

"Leah, I didn't mean it that way. We just have a lot to talk about. Look, let me go find out if the school is open. If I'm free today, maybe we could go for a drive and try to make some sense of this. If not, we could have dinner—out somewhere."

Taking my face in her hands, Leah trained her eyes on mine. "What's the matter? Are you afraid to be alone with me, afraid you might let yourself go again? Don't tell me you didn't feel something awesome last night. Alix, we were meant for this moment."

My hands reached for hers, and I was about to pull them away from my face and be mature and reasonable again, when Sgt. Gossett appeared seemingly out of nowhere. The guttural sound he made to clear his throat startled us apart. I was mortified that he'd found us standing there on the deck inches apart, only marginally dressed.

"Good morning, ladies. I'm sorry to interrupt, but frankly there's just never a good time for this." After taking off his hat, the officer pulled a paper out of his shirt pocket. "Ms. Leah Claire, also known as Lorelei Claire Hillyer, this is a warrant for your arrest for the murder of Meredith Jane Coates."

Gossett was interrupted by a stifled sob, that I recognized only afterwards as my own. He looked at me briefly, then returned to his litany of Mirandizing Leah: "You have the right to remain silent. You have the right to have an attorney...."

Softly Leah said, "It's okay, Sgt. Gossett. I understand most of my rights. Do they include a minute to put on some clothes?"

The officer nodded and moved aside to let Leah come down the stairs. He reached for her arm to hold onto her as he escorted her back to the main house, but then changed his mind and simply fell in step next to her. At the house, Officer Siebert waited next to the police cruiser. "We'll be out in a few minutes, Bobby. Tell the Fort Bragg station we're bringing her in."

I followed Gossett and Leah to the master bedroom where he let her go in only after checking doors and windows for possible escape routes. He watched while she selected a shirt, slacks and underwear, then allowed her to be alone in the room to dress as long as she didn't close the door completely.

As she got ready to be carted off, I glared at Gossett. "This is ridiculous, Sergeant. Leah is in no way capable of committing a murder. What possible motive could she have?"

He looked at me cautiously. "Well, ma'am, we had a couple of theories about that, and maybe as of this morning, we've got another." Almost as an afterthought, he drawled, "And didn't she practically lead you to that body?"

I couldn't begin to respond rationally to the insinuation that somehow Leah had to get rid of Meredith to be with me, or that she had somehow stage-managed our outing to lead me to discover

Meredith. I tried to speak, but every word turned into a sputter of rage and confusion before it reached my lips.

The door swung open, and Leah emerged, her face remarkably pale above a bright red cotton shirt and black slacks with a sharp crease. She gave me a look, but we were both afraid to exchange any meaningful words in front of the police. With a slight nod, she said, "I'll be in touch."

"No, wait. I'll come with you."

Her face melted into the slightest smile as she eyed me up and down standing there in flat slippers and a sky blue terry cloth robe. "I think not, Alix." Her voice was flat, neutral, as if she were speaking to someone who was just renting a cabin on her property. "If I can't call you later, I'll have my attorney do it. Look after the place while I'm gone, okay? Move your stuff into the main house if you'd like. At least you'll have access to the phone. It looks like I won't be using the place for a while."

"I'll be here."

Numbly I watched the police officers take Leah's arm and lead her to the cruiser. Gossett's hand instinctively reached for the steel handcuffs on his belt, but after a slight hesitation he simply opened the door and helped her into the back seat, guiding her head under the door frame almost tenderly. After they had driven away, I went to the kitchen to find the phone. Even if the school was open today, my class would not meet.

Leah had been right about the college. The storm had knocked out a major transformer and the power company didn't expect to get back on line until about noon. I was still in my robe and slippers heading back to the cabin to dress when I saw Veronica Battles charging down the drive from her place across the road.

"What happened? I saw the police here again. Have they found out who did it?"

I sighed with disgust, "Obviously they found out some things and added them up all wrong. They've arrested Leah."

"No shit? How interesting." In a gossipy tone, as if we were co-conspirators, she added, "D'ya suppose she could've done it?"

"If she did, she's been wasting her time in fund-raising. She could have made a fortune acting on stage. Leah was genuinely puzzled by Meredith's disappearance and devastated when I found the body."

"You found her? The police didn't mention who when they came to question us."

Apparently the police also never told Veronica who suggested she be questioned, because she kept up the mindless chatter like we were talking about something that had happened on an afternoon soap opera, not a murder that probably took place within a stone's throw of where we stood. I couldn't join in the small talk, even to placate and get rid of her, so I just said, "Us?"

"Yeah, Bert's here for vacation, but he didn't get to Fort Bragg until the day after Meredith disappeared so he couldn't tell the cops anything. It's just as well. He's in such a foul mood after losing that election."

I turned away trying to get back to the cabin to get dressed, tired of the prattle from this silly woman. But she grabbed my arm and pulled me around. I saw that her eyes were sad and distant. "What did she look like when you found her?"

"Veronica, for God's sake. I'd really rather forget what I saw."

She held onto my arm. "Please, I'd like to know. Was she, um, torn up very much? What was she wearing?"

Anything to get rid of this woman, I thought. I was willing to bet she studied the most grotesque photographs they could publish in the tabloid papers, too. "She was pale, not badly damaged, but some marine life had taken some nips on her face, and especially on her arms because of the sleeveless pullover she was wearing." I couldn't stand it. "I'm sorry, I really can't relive that moment. It's already come back to me in my nightmares."

For once she seemed genuinely subdued. "You're right. I shouldn't have bugged you that way. It must've been awful. That light green top *would* leave a lot of skin showing."

"Please, I really have to go, Veronica. She looked like hell no matter what she was wearing." As politely as I could, I removed her hand from my arm and headed back down the path to the cabin.

I fumed about Veronica's insensitivity while I dug a pair of jeans out of the narrow closet. The first shirt my hands found was a green one, and I pitched it clear across the room. "Damn fool lesbo-tourist!" Meredith's description of Veronica rang in my ears as I slipped into a royal blue turtleneck shirt and sat down to finish dressing. Sitting on the bed, I was distracted by the kitten who had been neglected in the furor. Assertively, she snatched at the toes of my socks as I pulled them on. "Okay, you. Just a minute. No need for all of us to go without breakfast."

I scooped up the little creature who had probably suffered her own loss because of someone's grievance against Meredith, and I admired her determination to thrive in spite of it. Stirring the formula and kibble until the kernels were soft, I thought about her spirit and made a decision. "I'm going to name you after one of my other favorite survivors. From now on, you're Genie."

Almost out of habit, I started to make coffee for myself, but my stomach lurched at the thought. Then I remembered there was no electricity for the coffee maker anyway. "So here we are," I addressed the kitten. "I'm dressed, you're fed, and Leah is gone." The sudden feeling of loss left my throat constricted, as if it were trying to stifle a scream. I gathered up a few essentials and the kitten's necessities and trudged back down to the main house. Leah had said I should stay there, but I wasn't ready to give up the thought that she would be back soon. I set Genie up in the second bathroom and closed the door so she wouldn't get lost in her new surroundings. And I waited.

About eleven a.m. the refrigerator motor kicking in told me the power was back on. Every time I passed the phone in the kitchen,

I wanted to reach for it to call the police station. But would my interest only put Leah in worse trouble? Gossett had seen us in a pretty intimate situation, and if Leah was trying to convince him otherwise, I could hurt her with a call.

By the afternoon, I was nearly frantic. What the hell were they doing with Leah? Had they let her call an attorney? Gossett seemed fairly restrained and laid back for a cop, but was it a ruse? Would he grill Leah mercilessly once he had her at the station? Grabbing my keys and wallet, I ran for the VW. The only place I'd felt serenity in the last week had been the Spread. I hoped Willow would have some wisdom to spare.

The Mandarin River was narrow, but the rain from last night's storm had already swelled its volume. I drove up to the gate and was about to jump out to open the latch, but Willow was already approaching from the other side. After I had parked, she took my arm. With a mystic smile, she said, "I've been waiting for you."

"What?" I was beginning to believe she just might be a witch.

The smile turned into an impish grin that rose all the way to her sparkling grey eyes. "Leah called here. She said you were bound to be worried. Erin's at the station with her now. Come on up to the house. I'll make us some tea."

Dumbly, I repeated, "Erin?" as I was led toward the ancient farmstead.

"Erin Reilly, the redhead. You met her yesterday at the ceremony. She's an attorney. She's been staying here about a year because she needed some healing, but she'll be moving on to a job up in Portland, Oregon after the first of the year. She's very good when she can believe in her client's innocence. And she believes in Leah."

Willow's melodic voice flowed over my exposed nerve endings, soothing my fears. When we were settled on a well-used sofa with sagging springs, she poured an aromatic herbal tea for us and said, "It will be alright. The Mother knows that Leah could not have taken Meredith's life. She will be safe."

I looked at her guardedly. "You don't believe innocent people are arrested, even convicted all the time?"

"I suppose they are, but not here, not with us watching. We won't let it happen, will we, Alix?" She squeezed my hand tightly.

"Willow, God, or the Goddess, knows, I don't want anything

to happen to Leah, but I don't know where to start."

Setting down her cup of tea, Willow said, "When Erin comes back we'll have a starting place, at least the same one the sheriff has." She left me then, after refilling my cup and setting a small plate of biscuits and a pot of jam next to me. I felt myself like a lost kitten who had just been taken in and given nourishment.

It was almost dark when Willow returned with Erin. The slender, almost frail-looking country girl had been replaced by a sharp-eyed, smartly dressed professional who set her briefcase on the coffee table next to the cold tea pot and snapped it open. Willow and I both leaned forward to hear what Erin had found out.

Standing tall, in her most adroit manner, she began, "Their case is circumstantial at best, but it wouldn't be the first time the wrong person got sent away on flimsy evidence."

When I stifled a sob, Willow said sharply to Erin, "We will not think that way."

Nodding her head in agreement, Erin conceded, "Okay, you're right. They've got a long way to go to prove their case."

Finally I asked, "What exactly have they got?"

"A murder weapon with her prints on it is probably the worst of it. They found traces of Meredith's blood and hair on the sledgehammer Leah had used to split firewood. There was a fair amount of blood soaked into the soil around the wood-cutting site, most of it covered with sawdust and wood chips. That's where they figure she was killed. Also, there was blood on a shirt they found hidden, to use their words, in her suitcase."

"A red plaid shirt? My God, I saw them take it. When I first saw Leah, she was splitting wood with a wedge and sledgehammer, and the shirt was on the ground. That blood must have already been there. She said it looked like the job had been left undone. Someone must have come up on Meredith while she was setting out tools for the kid who was supposed to split the wood."

Erin shook her head. "I know. Leah says the same thing, but the police found no other prints besides hers and Meredith's on the tools. The way the wood chips and split logs were dragged around, there's no way to prove anyone else was ever there.

"The other thing they found out is that Leah lied about Meredith's family. When they traced Meredith's father in Florida, they started to wonder if Leah was trying to avoid a fight over Meredith's estate. Police wisdom, such as it is, figures Leah wanted to cash in on Meredith's money and run away with..."

I couldn't sit still anymore. I got up and started to pace like a madwoman. "One goddammed night! They're going to pin a murder on her because Gossett saw us touching this morning?"

With a shrug, Erin said, "Something like that. Leah told me and told the cops why she chose not to mention Meredith's father, but they still think she didn't want any complications over the will."

"And that's it? They've put all of these so-called facts together and come up with the most stupid conclusion?" I wanted to take Gossett and Siebert and anyone else in law enforcement in the whole damn county and shake them senseless.

Erin's tone grew even more somber as she took my arm and sat me back down on the worn sofa next to Willow. "Not quite all of it, Alix. Leah told the police she arrived Saturday morning, but she bought gas just outside of town with a credit card on Friday night. That red Jeep with the Rainbow Nation wind sock was pretty easy to track down."

"What? But it's true. She didn't come to the house until Saturday. I was out photographing until ten o'clock. I would have seen her car when I got back. Where the hell was she?"

Gently Willow pressed her warm hands over my icy ones and said, "She was here. She was afraid to confront Meredith. As much as she felt she had to end things, she knew another Meredith, one that got hurt very easily. She went to a little gazebo down near the river to meditate."

"Then you can vouch for her—"

Willow cut me off. "No. I saw her when she came in on Friday night, but she was gone by Saturday morning. I couldn't swear to her whereabouts at the time of the murder."

I turned back to Erin, hoping she had something more encouraging to add. "Didn't anyone else see Leah in the morning, maybe before she showed up at the house?"

Rubbing her tired-looking face with both hands, Erin answered, "They haven't found anyone, Alix. Part of the problem is that the sea water flowing over Meredith's body, then ebbing away, has made it hard to determine a time of death. The way she was dressed seems to indicate she wasn't planning to be outside very long. The body temp, skin condition, everything was affected by the sea's motion. Their best guess is between six a.m. and noon on Saturday."

I felt like I was badgering Erin, who was only trying to help, but I couldn't stop asking questions. "Why have they honed in on Leah? Haven't they checked out anyone else? Parisi, or her business partner who was supposed to be in town that weekend, even Huberman deserves a look. The first words I heard out of his mouth were, 'I'm going to get even with her' or something to that effect."

Erin turned her palms up in a gesture of resignation. "The prints and the two lies really hurt Leah. What they can't figure out is why she'd leave a dead cat under Meredith's body."

I felt almost foolish asking about a feline autopsy, but it might mean something. "Any idea how the cat died?"

"They didn't go into detail, but apparently there was a bolo tie wrapped around its neck."

"Holy shit, Meredith had lost a bolo just a few days before the cat disappeared!"

"Probably was hers, but they all look so much alike, it would be hard to prove." Patiently, Erin continued to outline the sheriff's case against Leah, and we talked well into the night about his eagerness to wrap up the murder quickly, about anyone else who might have a motive to kill Meredith, and as we talked, I scratched out the beginning of a plan. There were three primary places Meredith might have lost a bolo tie—the school, Veronica's, and here at the Spread. I had already made a foolish stab at trying to find a killer amid this diverse and spiritual group, and I dismissed immediately the thought that any of them, even the volatile Casey Watson, would harm a helpless animal out of spite.

That left the other two locations that needed looking into. I would have to swallow my pride and apologize to Veronica and get back into Huberman's good graces, but anything was worth it to get Leah free. Too much had been left unsaid between us, but my reaction to the danger she was in exposed my raw feelings for her. Until she was safe, I wouldn't be able to think rationally about our future or lack of one.

I finally got up to return to the house. Willow put a warm

hand on my arm. "You're welcome to stay the night. We do have some extra beds."

"Thanks, but I've got to get back to Genie." At her quizzical look, I explained, "She's the kitten of the dead cat found with Meredith. She was born in the woodshed near the cabin, even though Meredith refused to claim ownership. The mother was missing for a day or two before Meredith died. I've been feeding her."

Willow smiled. "Why Genie? Did she come out of a bottle?"

"I named her this morning when she spoke up for herself. I named her after my favorite photographer, Imogene Cunningham. She was taking pictures when men didn't expect women to do much of anything outside of the kitchen or the bedroom." I turned to Erin. "Will I be able to see Leah?"

Erin nodded, "I'll be seeing her again tomorrow afternoon. If you'd like, I'll pick you up at the college and take you with me into the conference room. If you want to see her, we'd better do it soon before they move her over the hill."

"Over the hill?"

"Since the murder occurred outside of the town limits, it's strictly a county case. County prisoners are usually taken directly to the jail in Ukiah, but Gossett and Siebert had another call. Some guy found dead in a huge marijuana patch near Westport. As a courtesy, the Fort Bragg city jail will hold county prisoners for a short time, but then they get transferred to Ukiah."

"Ukiah? Isn't that over sixty miles away?"

"Sixty miles from town. More like seventy-five from here. I don't think my pleas about hardship for the defense will hold out too long, but I'll try to keep her on the coast as long as I can."

I started to say 'thank you' but my voice cracked against my will. I squeezed Erin's hand, accepted a hug from Willow and left. *You said it, Nicholson. One goddammed night—and almost twenty years of wondering what had become of the dark-haired girl in the pictures.* Now I was wondering what was to become of us both.

E arly Wednesday morning, I contacted Connie and asked her to take over the class for me in case I got to school late. I put on a red pullover sweatshirt with a hood, grey sweatpants and my best running shoes. I wanted to look the part of a committed jogger. I trotted slowly past Veronica's driveway several times before she came out to retrieve the morning paper. As I saw her approach I went into my best imitation of an aerobic walking pace and stopped at her mailbox just as she bent down to get the paper.

With a smile I hoped looked more genuine than it felt, I called, "Veronica, I was hoping I'd see you this morning. I wanted to apologize for snapping at you yesterday. The sheriff's men had just left, and their attitude really pissed me off. I'm sorry you got in the way of my explosion."

Veronica Battles was no pushover. She looked at me warily, pulling her long, flowered-print housecoat around her as if for protection. Her pale green eyes narrowed to mere slits. "Yeah, well, I s'pose it was a shock, especially since I heard you two didn't even have time to cover up—your bodies, that is."

God—news sure traveled fast in a small town. I bit my lip to keep back what I wanted to say and hung my head slightly. I needed to get close to this woman if I was to find out if she was a killer. Feigning embarrassment, I said, "It was a surprise. Actually, Leah and I knew each other a very long time ago, and for a lot of reasons, we weren't able to act on our feelings then. Perhaps it was something we needed to get out of our systems." *Yeah, right, Nicholson. Now that your first night with Leah is out of your system, you're aching for another dose.*

"Anyway," I added, "I just wanted to say I was sorry. I'm sure, since you've known Meredith for a while, you would want to know some things, like if she suffered or whatever."

She tilted her head slightly. "Thanks. It's hard to believe she's really gone. I keep expecting her to come whipping out of that driveway in her Ford to pick up clients and close a deal." Absently, Veronica twisted the rolled-up *San Francisco Chronicle* she held in her hand. "Always got real excited just before one of her maneuvers paid off. She sure knew how to make a buck."

Listening to admiration for a dead woman's money-making ability seemed utterly inane, but apparently it was the note I needed to engage Veronica's interest because she went on to say, "I remember hearing her talk about some deal to buy the land that the college is on for future development, then lease it back to the school until the new owners could get all the permits and building plans in order. Claimed the school'd be gone within five years."

"Vernie, where's that paper? I been waitin' for ten minutes. My coffee's almost gone." Striding up the driveway was a large, heavy-set man in blue shorts cut just above the knee and a black tank top. He beat me in the height department by at least four inches, which made him six-three or more. I guessed his weight at close to two-hundred-fifty pounds, but he moved with some speed.

"Who's this?" he snapped.

"Bert, hold on. I was just on my way back. This is Alix Nicholson. She teaches at the college, lives in the cabin behind Meredith's house."

Bert Battles looked at me, nodded his head with a slight sneer and snatched the paper away from Veronica rudely. "I thought you wanted me to take you shopping in Santa Rosa today. Better move your ass, 'cause I don't want to spend the hottest part of the day in the car." He marched back down the drive, and Veronica turned to follow him, saying, "It gets so warm in the valley even at this time of the year. Bert hates driving in a hot car, and he can't stand air conditioning."

From the look of him, I guessed Bert hated just about everything, including Veronica.

✦ ✦ ✦ ✦ ✦

Connie was setting up the photo chemistry in the darkroom with the help of two other students when I arrived. Class was scheduled to start within fifteen minutes. She eyed me with concern, and we left the others to finish setting up. She took my arm and led me into the empty classroom. "You look like you haven't slept in days," she said gently.

"I did...a little, last night. Monday night and most of Tuesday were just a blur, lost days...I was just so angry and frustrated. Finally, I got to sleep last night, but I couldn't handle staying in Meredith's bedroom so I used the futon in the study. Maybe I should just go back to the cabin, but at least there's a phone in the main house."

"It isn't Meredith's room anymore, Alix. She's moved on, remember that."

"Thanks, and thanks for covering for me. I'm beginning to feel a little guilty taking a salary for this term. I'm not sure I've taught anyone much of anything."

Connie shook her head. "You have, don't worry. And there will be time for more learning when Leah is free."

"I hope you're right." I thought back to Washington, D.C. and my friend, Mac MacDowell, who had been terrified when someone she thought she loved had been arrested for murder. "I feel so helpless; I'm grasping at straws hoping one of them will lead me to the truth."

Other students were starting to arrive so Connie said softly, "Erin says you're going with her to the jail today. Maybe between the three of you, the right straw will reveal itself." We separated then, and I worked the rest of the morning helping students select negatives to print, suggesting ways to burn in detail or dodge out dark areas, and wondering if anything I told them made any sense.

About thirty minutes before the class ended, I called the students together to critique prints they had made for an earlier assignment about capturing people as they celebrated Halloween, which had been the previous weekend. I wanted to catch them before they tried manipulating their work with filters or dodging and burning techniques, which can be used to minimize the flaws in some negatives.

Feeling a little more like a real teacher after several in-depth critiques of their work, I headed for the parking lot to meet Erin. I rode with her to the county prison facility, a new one-story building at the south end of town. Erin, again smartly dressed in a cream-colored wool skirt suit with a navy blue blouse, briskly identified herself to the custodian and got permission for me to accompany her into the attorney's conference room. We sat at a small table, waiting for the guard to bring Leah in. Erin pulled off her suit jacket with relief. "I thought I was ready to get back into these costumes and play act for the legal system. Maybe I was wrong."

"Having second thoughts about going to Portland?"

"More like cold feet at leaving the Spread," Erin conceded with a sigh. "It is such a haven, but I suppose I can't hide there forever."

"And who were you hiding from?"

"Myself, mostly. At least the self that believed even the guilty deserve the best defense. My law professors kept saying, 'That's what makes our system so great.' I believed it enough to convince a jury of twelve good women and men that my client was innocent of raping a fourteen-year-old girl. Along the way, I had forgotten that this great system was made for, and by, men. Six months after I got him off, my ex-client strangled a sixteen-year-old girl while he was raping her. I felt like I had aimed him at her." Her bright blue eyes turned dark and filled with pain.

I couldn't find words to reply to that kind of anguish, but I admired Erin having the courage to face the world again, and was impressed by the miracle of healing to be found among a circle of loving women. The quiet in the room was broken by the heavy metal door creaking open. Leah was led into the room by a male guard. She was handcuffed and wore a bright orange prison jumpsuit. We both eyed each other, but by design our gazes never met.

Without hesitation, Erin stood up, grabbed the cuffs and demanded, "These have to go. I'm an officer of the court, too. There's no need for restraints."

While the guard unlocked the shackles, I sat leaning on the table with my hands clenched in front of me to keep from reaching for Leah. When the guard was gone, Erin took Leah's arm and led her to the chair which was at right angles to mine, then settled herself across from me. It took only a few seconds to find Leah's trembling hand under the table. I gripped it hard as she finally looked at me and smiled. Without sound, she mouthed the words, "I've missed you."

I nodded and was trying to find my own voice when Erin interrupted. "Leah, have you thought of anything else that might help your case? Did you stop for breakfast or coffee or see anyone after you left the Spread and before you went to the house and found Meredith missing?"

With a shake of her head, Leah sighed, "No, I didn't stop anywhere people might have seen me. I did walk at Seaside Beach that morning on my way south to Meredith's. I was having a lot of trouble figuring out how to approach her, and..." She paused and dropped her eyes. "...and I was terrified about coming face to face with Alix again. I knew she couldn't be the way I remembered her, but I'd lived with that memory for such a long time..."

Erin cut her off. "Maybe we'd better not get into that right now. And when you drove up to the house, you didn't see anything unusual?"

"Nothing except what I already told you: Meredith's car was gone, the wood-splitting tools were tossed in a pile of chips, and there was a stack of logs, cut into fireplace lengths waiting to be split."

"Erin," I broke in, "haven't the police even considered anyone else? Everyone I've mentioned Pete Parisi to tells me he's not dangerous, but the man wears a knife at his belt, and he threatened me."

Erin smiled at me indulgently. "Alix, Pete's a fisherman. Take a walk around Noyo Harbor sometime. Half the men you see will have a knife on their belts, the others will have one in a back pocket or sitting next to them on a boat. Besides, Meredith wasn't stabbed, remember?" At my blush, her voice softened, "I know you desperately want someone else to be guilty—"

"Someone else is guilty, Erin."

"I know that, all three of us know that, and maybe it is Pete Parisi, but the sheriff needs some solid evidence before he can go after anyone. What he's got on Leah, even though it is circumstantial, would make a reasonably sound case, if she were guilty. Since she's not, we'll have to find equally compelling evidence against someone else."

"Leah, can you explain how you could have gone to work on that wood pile and not noticed blood on the ground?"

"I don't know. The wood chips and sawdust looked fresh to me."

Erin's eyebrows shot up. "Wood chips? Sawdust? Maybe that's it. Didn't you tell me some kid was supposed to split that wood? Meredith certainly wouldn't have done it herself if she'd hired someone."

Leah exclaimed, "That's right!"

"But you didn't find the chainsaw out there, did you?"

"No, just the hand tools."

Erin stood up and started to pace. "That's it! Whoever killed Meredith spread the chips and sawdust to cover up the blood, maybe even took some away. The killer was trying to mask the fact a murder had been committed as long as possible. He must have overlooked some of the blood, and that's what ended up on your shirt. You said you were perspiring when you took it off and tossed it on the ground. The damp shirt picked up some of the blood the killer missed." Triumphantly she slapped her yellow pad on the table. "I knew the amount of blood they found on your shirt wasn't consistent with you having smashed in Meredith's head, then moving her body. That shirt would have been soaked with her blood."

Leah turned pale somewhere in the midst of Erin's working out her conclusions. I wanted to hold her and tell her everything would be all right, but I settled for stroking the back of her hand with my thumb. Now that Erin was back in top form, her questions came faster, her style more demanding. "What kind of chainsaw did Meredith have?"

"Electric, I think."

"Do you know if there's an outside outlet next to that wood pile?"

"No, I have no idea."

Turning to me, Erin said, "That's you're first assignment. Check out the side of the house where Meredith was killed. If there's no outlet, find out where it is and try to determine where she would have cut logs, if she did."

Leah shook her head. "Meredith wasn't that kind of dyke. She'd just as soon have the firewood delivered and dropped next to the fireplace. The only reason she had a chainsaw was that it came with the property. She kept it in case she needed to move a fallen branch or sapling near the house." Leah realized what she had just said. "Of course! Meredith wouldn't have had uncut logs on the property. There was no logical reason for there to be sawdust among the wood chips."

"Erin," I said with excitement, "about a week before Meredith disappeared, a tree came down or was cut down so that it fell right across her driveway. We nearly smashed into it coming back to the house from the party at the Spread. The very next morning she had someone come by and cut it into chunks with a gasoline-powered saw. It was probably the same kid she had hired to split the logs. I watched him for a while. He cut the tree up right in the driveway. It wouldn't have made sense to move it, then cut it up."

Erin was in high gear now. "Alright, you check out the driveway and the wooded areas next to it and see if there's any sawdust there. I'm convinced the killer used it to cover up evidence of a murder on the property."

The flurry of excited discussion over, the three of us lapsed into silence, trying to come up with another clue to renew the trail we were blazing toward a murderer.

After a moment, Erin looked at us and winked. "I'll go tell the guard I'm done. You've got maybe thirty seconds, a minute, tops." She closed the door softly behind her, and Leah and I were in each other's arms.

In a gently mocking voice, Leah said, "And what was it you were trying to tell me when we were so rudely interrupted, dear Alix?"

My voice rough with emotion, I murmured, "It's not important, now. Maybe it never was." I kissed her lightly and cradled her dark hair in my hand. I wanted to taste deep into her mouth, her tongue—but I was afraid if I started exploring there, I'd want to taste her everywhere. As we separated, I took her face in my hands as she had done mine the night she first kissed me. "Soon you'll be out of here, and we'll have all the time we need to figure out what's going to happen to us."

We stood like that until we heard the warning creak of the doorknob that gave us time to disengage before Erin and the guard entered the room. As he placed the handcuffs on Leah, we stole one last glance at each other. I hoped my eyes said that I'd find out who really killed Meredith...and I wished I could believe it.

I was tired of everyone telling me I was wrong about Pete Parisi and decided to have a chat with him myself. I remembered hearing that his shop opened at six a.m. to accommodate fishermen leaving at daybreak. I planned to be there early, too. Thursday morning, I put on a pair of old, soft jeans, a boat-neck black pullover, my denim jacket and ankle-high, hard-soled boots. I hoped I looked tougher than I felt. I grabbed my copies of the shots I'd taken of his pickup parked alongside Meredith's car, and pointed my bus toward Noyo Harbor.

As I headed for Parisi's shop in the harbor, I rehearsed my excuse for being there and hoped I wouldn't tremble. My last encounter with Parisi remained far too vivid to make this assignment a piece of any kind of cake.

Pete Parisi was busy with a customer when I stepped into his cluttered shop. The smells of brine and fish were strong near the bait tanks, but otherwise the shop was clean, if cluttered. Fishing poles of varying sizes and weights were mounted on a rail at the back of the store, while a glass case showcased an array of reels. The walls were lined with pegboards which displayed the accessories of fishing: lures, baskets, floats and the like. And fish nets and buoys of all kinds hovered above my head.

As the customer left with his purchase, Parisi turned his attention to me. "Can I help..." he started, then recognized me. "You! What d'you want in here?" His voice was harsh, but the tone was more of surprise than anger.

I shrugged innocently. "Christmas is coming, and I thought you might have something here I could send to my dad in Missouri."

"That so?" His eyes never left me as I moved closer to the

counter he was standing behind.

"Yes. I've come to like this town a lot, and I agree with what you said about chain stores killing local businesses. So when I saw the chance to support a local shop, I..." My voice trailed off as I swallowed the part of the statement that was an outright lie. It was true that I did see the exceptional nature of this part of the coast, and did want to help sustain local shopkeepers, but Parisi's business would not have been my first choice. And I think he knew it.

I thought I detected a slight flush in his face at my reference to our encounter on Pudding Creek Beach, but it was hard to tell behind the stubble of his beard.

"Missouri, is it? Figured you for an inlander." His stare challenged me to stay, and when I did, I think he decided to join the charade he knew I was acting out. "Whatja have in mind, lady?"

"Well, I'm not quite sure. I'm just tired of sending the usual things like ties he never wears, and shirts in my favorite colors, instead of his. I know he likes fishing. My stepmother mentions his being off on one trip or another when she writes."

"Boat or stream?"

"I beg your pardon?"

"He fish off a boat or standing in a stream?"

"I...I...I guess I don't know."

Parisi turned away from a box he was about to open. "Guess that leaves out waders."

Nervously I nodded. "Maybe I'll just look around for a bit. Maybe something will jump out at me."

A slight smile played around Parisi's mouth as he gestured at his inventory. "Take yer time."

After a few minutes of stalling while I browsed around the store trying to remember anything about my father's hobby, I picked up a sturdy tan cotton vest with a dozen or more small pockets lined up on both sides of the breast pieces. Taking my selection to Parisi, I was startled when a fat, purring tortoiseshell cat jumped in front of me onto the counter. Parisi stroked her absently as he moved her aside.

"Don't pay her no mind. She adopted this place years ago when she wasn't no bigger than a tadpole herself. Guess the smells tempted her, and she's kept the place free of mice and fish guts ever since."

Parisi reached for the vest, but my eyes were still on the cat. "Didn't scare ya, did she?"

"No, no," I said. "It's just her markings. She looks a lot like the one they found on the beach with Mere—with Ms. Coates. Of course, that one was a scrawny stray, not sleek like—"

"Spinner. That's what she's called. I used to take 'er home with me sometimes, but she and my old dog, Copper, never did hit it off." He started ringing up the vest, then stopped as if he'd just heard my remark about the other tortie. "Ya say they found one like 'er with that real estate woman, Coates. Peculiar, most cats don't much like bein' on the sand, messes up their toes or somethin'."

The man was either genuinely unaware of how the cat was found, or a very good actor. With my perceptions clouded from so badly wanting to find someone other than Leah to blame for Meredith's murder, I wasn't sure which he was.

"This one was dead, stuffed under her body," I said, flatly, trying to evoke a response.

"Damn peculiar, then," he said, completing the sale. "Think ya made a good choice. Must be pretty close to your dad if you can figure out what he'd want so quick."

It was my turn to feel color rising in my cheeks. What I had with my father and stepmother was more a truce than a relationship. Despite some overtures from them in the last few years, I'd managed to stay pissed for eighteen years over their abrupt retreat from me when I got in trouble with the school board over the nude pictures Lorie and Cathy had shot so long ago.

I picked up my package and the change from my purchase. Our business transaction over, I groped for a way to continue my inquiry. Through the storefront window I could see a portion of the bluffs that sheltered the mouth of the Noyo River as it spilled out to sea. Pointing at a spot where the foliage was broken and twisted, I asked innocently, "Is that where they found her car?"

Parisi came around the counter then and grabbed my arm, not violently, but hard enough to turn me toward him. "Look, Ms. Nicholson, I didn't kill that woman. Not sayin' the thought hadn't crossed my mind, but it wouldn't have done no good. So she's gone, but soon enough there'll be six more like her lined up tellin' folks how much money they can get for their places. I'm gonna keep fightin' 'em, but I'm gonna do it so's they can't keep comin' at us. I'm gonna make them fix the laws to protect this harbor."

Defiantly, I pulled my arm out of his grip and snatched the envelope of photographs from my back pack. Waving one of the 8x10 black-and-white prints at him, I spat out, "If you're so damned innocent, how come you were stalking Meredith for weeks after you threatened her at her house?"

Parisi walked away from me, waving his hand brusquely. "Yer crazy, lady. I ain't got time for any o' that kind of shit. I still got a business to run." With a flick of his wrist, he snatched the photo out of my hand and examined it in the bright sunlight streaming through the shop window. After a moment, he snorted scornfully and shoved the print into my body, crumpling it. "That ain't my truck. Same make and model, but mine's got a guard rail all around to keep Copper from jumpin' outta the truck so easy." At my disbelieving stare, he added, "Take a look for yourself. It's parked right out back."

I pulled out the rest of the shots and shuffled through them one by one. Without responding to Parisi, I flung the door open, making the signal bell jangle violently as I ran around to the back. It was true. Not only was there no guard rail on the white truck in my photos, there were other subtle differences as well. The rusting patterns didn't match, and, most convincing, there was one shot which included the license plate. It didn't match Parisi's truck tag either.

My heart fell then because I finally did believe him, and that left one less suspect in my search to get Leah out of jail.

I turned to find Parisi behind me. For a guy with a bum leg, he could sure move pretty silently. My eyes down, I murmured, "I'm sorry, Mr. Parisi. I won't bother you anymore."

Before I reached my car, Parisi called to me one more time. "Thanks for the business, lady, and I'm sorry if I scared ya that day on the beach, but I was damn mad."

I leaned back in the comfortable VW seat, worn to fit my body over the past five years, and let out a deep breath. So Parisi was most likely off my list. And that meant there was a new job to do—finding out who *did* own that other white Chevy truck. But right now it was time to get to my photo lab.

✦ ✦ ✦ ✦ ✦

After another day of seriously working with my lab students, advising them on the prints they were making, I was beginning to regain some of my old excitement about the possibilities of darkroom work. I used to let my dear friend and colleague Brian Bellamy bring life to my negatives because he loved manipulating prints as much as I loved the hunt for the images. But Brian had died over two years ago, and since then I had looked upon printing photographs as a chore. Whatever came out of this semester of residency, I would always be grateful for putting the joy back into making finished prints of the images I captured on film.

It was Thursday and I was relieved that my work week was over. Now I could concentrate on finding the proof we needed to convince the sheriff's department and the district attorney that someone other than Leah had killed Meredith. With Parisi apparently out of the picture, the most logical, if not the most likely, place to start was with Huberman. I checked down the hall in his classroom, but it was empty.

Striding across campus to the administration building, I rehearsed my excuse for seeing him, but as soon as I stepped into his office I could tell it was vacant, too. In fact, it appeared that all the offices in the narrow, railroad-car-style building were empty. I knew staff members often left early due to the few demands on their time outside of classwork. I was almost out the door when I heard a familiar name from an angry voice. "I know the Coates woman is gone, but there's still her partner in Sacramento. He can help us close this deal."

After a pause, the voice grew louder, more irate. "No, I won't forget about it. This was our chance to make some real money instead of waiting for tuitions and gifts to trickle in." The telephone receiver hit the base with a bang.

I decided the voice had to be coming from Mark Sutter's office at the opposite end of the hall from Huberman's office. He must have been very agitated for his voice to carry that far. I knew very little about him except what Huberman and Meredith had told me when I arrived. I had managed to do a little research on his sister, Sonya Abbott. Much older than her half-brother, she had a reputation as a gifted sculptor and used it to found a private teaching studio on the Pudding Creek bluff nearly fifty years ago. After World War II, the curriculum was expanded to include other art disciplines and a board was formed to administer the college. As president and her sole surviving heir,

Sutter received a dividend from the school's proceeds annually.

As I pretended to study the bulletin board on the wall across from Huberman's office, I listened to determine if he was going to call someone else or reconnect with the party he had cut off. I was about to give up and head home when Huberman approached me from behind. "Can I help you with something, Alix?"

I turned to him with a benign smile. "Actually, yes. I was wondering if, as a temporary employee, I had access to the school's vehicle. I'd like to take my advanced class to the museum in Ukiah. They're opening a documentary photographic exhibit on the local Native American populations from the last hundred years." When Huberman seemed to be mulling over the idea, I added, "I feel like my class has missed so much time, what with the power outage, and my preoccupation these last few days with Meredith's murder."

That seemed to persuade him. With a firm nod of his head, Huberman said, "Certainly. I can arrange to get you the key and a fuel credit card for a field trip. I'm glad to see you're doing better these days, Alix."

"Well," I admitted, "it wasn't easy realizing that someone had killed a woman just a few hundred feet from where I was sleeping."

Huberman looked startled. "I imagine that was a shock. I hadn't recalled that the cabin was that close to the house. But then, if she was killed inside, you might not have heard anything even if you were awake."

"That's true; However, the police seem to think that whoever killed Meredith did it outside, near the wood pile."

Huberman looked at me warily, as if waiting for my reaction to his next remark. "I see. You talk about 'whoever killed Ms. Coates,' but don't the police have a suspect in custody?"

I almost blurted out a fierce denial of Leah's guilt, but that would have satisfied Huberman's curiosity too much. Probably he, too, had heard about our state of dress and undress when the police arrived, and confirming his suspicions about my personal stake in the matter would make it hard to coax any gossip out of him. As coolly as I could manage, I said, "I wouldn't be surprised to see her released soon. I hear she has a very good attorney. Then the sheriff will have to dig a little deeper."

Huberman's eyebrows raised slightly as he waited for more

information from me, but it was his turn to give. Drawing him a little away from Sutter's door, I said conspiratorially, "It sounds like your boss is a little upset today."

"Boss?" Huberman snorted. "The man's a lowbrow. He and his real estate broker thought they could sell the land that Pacific Arts stands on and not get caught. If the land interests were separated from the school, a new owner could close the college if it fell into debt and couldn't honor the lease. But Meredith Coates was his agent and now that she's gone, the buyers aren't nearly as interested. She had a way of getting concessions and waivers from regulatory commissions that will be hard to duplicate."

His smile was triumphant, but I wasn't sure if it was also sinister. I thanked Huberman for the use of the school's passenger van, but before leaving the campus, I returned to the arts building and the tiny department office shared by all the art faculty. I locked up some of my books in the cabinet I was assigned and checked the pigeonhole mailbox with my name printed below it. With a jolt I remembered that Meredith would have a mail box and cabinet space as well. Had the police known about it and checked it out, or were they so preoccupied with the evidence they found at the house they neglected looking elsewhere?

I walked quickly back to the administration building where the business department's office was. As a pilot project the department only rated a halftime secretary, and she was long gone. I pulled open the office door and found Huberman stooped over a lower cabinet. At my entrance, he straightened up immediately and smoothed down his brown tweed suit jacket. "Why, Ms. Nicholson, Alix, I thought you had left the campus."

"I was about to," I stalled, casting my eyes around for a reason to be there, "but I wanted to leave a note for Mr. Collins, the computer teacher. I was hoping he could spare some time to discuss a new filing and storage program I've thought about buying for my photo archives." I stood in the middle of the office digging in my over-the-shoulder book bag for paper and pencil to write an imaginary note, hoping Huberman would get the hell out. I won the standoff, and Huberman left the cramped office with a curt nod.

I closed the office door and went to look at the cabinet Huberman had been squatting next to. As I suspected, it was Meredith's.

It appeared as if either the police or someone else had broken into the locker because there was a hole in the wood cabinet door where the lock should have been. Two of Meredith's books remained in the locker, and I picked up the first one and flipped through the pages looking for anything of use. The second one had two pieces of 8½x11 paper folded in half, the long end sticking out of the top. Some notes for a class on escrow were scribbled at the top of the outside sheet. I pulled the paper out and opened it up. The inside page was a photocopy of a message. In bold, block letters it read HANDS OFF PAC ARTS, OR YOU'LL DISAPPEAR, TOO!

Was this what Huberman had been trying to find? Had he made the cat disappear as a warning to Meredith? And had he been waiting for the situation to cool off, comfortable in his guilt, until I suggested Leah might get off easily? Had I nudged him into making a move to retrieve it? Returning the paper to the book, I knew I had contaminated any fingerprint evidence there might have been, but the threat remained real. I was afraid to leave anything for Huberman to get his hands on, so I slipped the books and notes into my bag, then turned to inspect Meredith's mail box.

Several bulletins were shoved into the letter-sized cubbyhole high in the stack, most dated after her death and inserted no doubt by some bored student intern who was simply told to give one to every faculty member. I could easily remove the sheets of paper, but I had to stand on tiptoe to look all the way to the back of the mailbox. Something hard and lumpy had been pushed all the way to the back as each day's bulletin had been delivered. And since the box was deep and narrow, I had to wiggle my fingers to the back to retrieve it. Staring at it in the palm of my hand, I recognized it as a silver slide for a bolo tie—obviously custom made because its design was an initial M superimposed over the initial C.

She had apparently left or lost the bolo tie and slide here on campus, and the finder had slipped it into her box, only to have someone take the tie. Someone a bit shorter than I was, most likely; someone who couldn't fumble around for the slide without attracting attention. I felt like I was getting closer to some answers, but worried that, although I was finding some clues, I was also contaminating them with my own fingerprints and moving them from where they were found in my eagerness to get Leah free.

I was beginning to believe Huberman had not only abducted the tortie, but probably killed her as well. But what proof was there to corroborate that he had also murdered Meredith? And why would he have taken the bolo tie? This just wasn't enough evidence to take to the police, but Erin needed to know what I had found.

That evening, as I reported my skirmish with Parisi and my findings at the college to Erin, she stood next to the fireplace in Meredith's sitting room weighing the heavy bolo slide in her hand. Thoughtfully, she shook her head. "It's okay, Alix. It would not have mattered much if the police had found this stuff. The note's a photo-copy, so probably only Meredith's fingerprints are on it. She must have made a copy and left it in her locker to use against Huberman at some point. My guess is Huberman wrote the note, snatched the animal, and when Meredith wasn't scared off the school land deal, he strangled the poor creature and was leaving the remains when Meredith caught him. He panicked and pushed her into a fall that made her head strike the sledgehammer, or he grabbed the tool and swung wildly. Then he decided to move the body before you got up so it would look like she had taken off on her own."

Through her intelligent, animated eyes I could see the attorney's mind formulating a plausible case against Roald Huberman. Erin left the spot near the fireplace and picked up a folded manila envelope she had brought with her. With a crooked grin, she said, "This is the medical examiner's report. I've been carrying it around in my back pocket—I haven't gotten used to lugging my briefcase every-where yet." She sat down next to me and studied the papers. They looked well-worn, and her eyes moved quickly from page to page. She obviously had spent much time on this report already and knew what she was looking for.

She returned the report to the envelope and stared into space for a moment. "The report is inconclusive as to whether the injury was a striking blow or a fall. Those are hard to determine anyway, and with the damage done to her from the wave action in the cave, it's almost impossible. Maybe Huberman didn't even know she was ex-pecting Leah. Another few days in that sea cave and the body would have been so badly decomposed, battered or gnawed on that it would have been much harder to determine cause of death. Perhaps he was even expecting the tide to carry it out to sea, and it might have, except that her belt caught on a jagged rock protruding from the sand."

Breaking her train of thought, Erin looked at me and shrugged. "It could have happened that way, but there's not a shred of real proof. What really frosts me is that you were on the property and that neighbor across the road is pretty damn nosy, but the murderer got away without anyone seeing or hearing anything."

With a sigh, I said, "I guess Veronica and I are about to become better friends." I didn't relish spending any more time than necessary blathering with this insensitive woman who talked about Meredith as if she were away on a long trip rather than dead. But it was important to find out if she knew anything about who came and went on the Saturday morning Meredith disappeared.

Returning to the fireplace, Erin picked up the poker and jabbed at the logs. "I'll also find someone to run the license plate on that truck through the Department of Motor Vehicles, Alix, but there's something else we need to talk about. The sheriff's department moved Leah this morning to the county jail in Ukiah." I opened my mouth to protest, but Erin continued. "I told you it would happen. We've been lucky that the county couldn't afford to spare a deputy to transport her until now. It doesn't change much except that it will be harder for me to meet with her, and almost impossible for me to bring you with me when I do."

I felt a cold fist in my chest. "Dammit! Will I be able to see her at all?"

"Of course. Even though she's being held on a capital crime, she's innocent until a jury says otherwise. She has the right to visitors, but visiting times are severely limited, except for the accused's attorney. And a guard will be close by while you're together. There's a bail hearing on Friday, but I'm not counting on very much help from the D.A.'s office on setting reasonable bail. All of Meredith's assets have been frozen pending Leah's trial, so she has no access to those funds. Without them, I don't think we can make bail. I'm sorry."

While I sat silently gazing into the fire, Erin sat down next to me. "Alix, I need to know what is between you and Leah. One moment she passes it off as a simple affair, the next she's talking like you are a couple and have plans for the future."

"I don't know what's between us, as you put it. I had known her barely a week before the police carted her off. And when they came to arrest her, I was about to tell her we didn't have a future. We had made love the night before, and she clearly had deep feelings for me. I'm having trouble accepting that as grown-up love when even she admits those feelings started when she was fourteen years old, for God's sake."

Her eyes sad, Erin said, "Well, even if you don't know what you're feeling, the cops seem to think they do. The reason I'm expecting the law to request a high bail is that Leah is not a local resident with ties to the community and, in fact, has an apartment in the Bay Area, plus because of her relationship with you, they are contending that she is a flight risk."

I leaped off the couch in a rage and shouted, "What the hell? They're nuts! How could they possibly think Leah would jump bail, or that I'd help a fleeing fugitive?"

Erin took me by the shoulders and turned me to face her. She was even taller than me and looked down at me like a child. Also as if I was a petulant child, she took my chin in her hand and asked, "But isn't there something you're not saying, Alix?"

My anger deflated, I said softly, "Alright, what I'm not saying is that since they took her away, I've felt as empty as when my best friend, Brian, died. I want to dismiss it as fear for her, as sadness about Meredith, even as longing for another night of torrid sex. What I'm afraid of is that I'm beginning to fall in love with her, too."

"Or is it that you are afraid you were in love with that four-teen-year-old all those years ago?" When I couldn't answer her, Erin twisted her lips into a knowing grin. "Not to worry, Alix. It's only against the law if you had acted on those feelings for a minor."

I got up and walked to the window. I could see the skylights of the cabin catching the rays of a setting sun. I wanted to be back there, to have Meredith knocking on my door for a cup of coffee, to still be wondering who this woman Leah was. "It's not that—" I started. "Well, maybe it's partly that, but it's also that we've made lives for ourselves two thousand fucking miles apart. I can't see Leah wanting to come back to the Midwest, and I'm awfully settled back home in Iowa. It's just too goddammed complicated."

"Have you told her that?"

"I can't, not while the goddammed cops have her."

"And when she's free?"

"I don't know what I'll tell her then. Hell, I don't even know what she'll want of me by then."

Erin picked up her notes and the things I had found in Meredith's locker and rose to go. "You may have only known her a week, my friend, but you're already picking up her language habits."

With a groan, I said, "Oh, damn," and saw Erin to the door.

The next day I checked out the Battles's house every hour or so, trying to find a way to get Veronica Battles into conversation without Bert around. But every time I started up their driveway, I could hear him mowing the lawn or see him bent over his rose garden, deadheading spent blossoms, pulling soil up around the base of the rose bushes for protection from the cooler weather, or trimming the edges of the flower beds.

It seemed ironic that he had stayed away from the coast all fall, enmeshed in his union election campaign, while the roses were still in high bloom, but came up just in time to put them to rest for the winter. In truth, even the notion that Bert Battles was a gardener and rose fancier seemed incongruous.

Finally, on Saturday, I had to abandon my pursuit of Veronica for the day to take my class to the museum in Ukiah. The drive in the school's twelve-passenger van was less than relaxing. The cumbersome vehicle swayed excessively on the winding two-lane road over the mountains from Fort Bragg, and I grew increasingly tense driving this unfamiliar vehicle on such a treacherous highway. About halfway to Willits, where we would pick up the state highway, I pulled over to let a long line of cars pass, and Connie tapped my arm. "Want me to drive for a while?"

"I don't think the school would approve. I'm sure their insurance wouldn't cover any driver except the instructor."

With a gently mocking laugh, Connie said, "If I drive, there won't be any need for an insurance company to get involved. I used to work at the hospital in Willits and drove this route every day." Several of the students behind us voiced agreement with Connie, and I reluctantly slid over to the passenger seat. It wasn't an appropriate thing for a teacher to do, but I decided the group was far safer and more likely to get to Ukiah promptly in Connie's capable hands. After a few minutes of watching Connie cut the curves just slightly to minimize the swing of the suspension, I knew I had made the right decision. It took a certain skill on the switchbacks to avoid making every passenger carsick—and I didn't have it.

The county museum was in a modern one-story building. In addition to the ancient photographs of the Pomo Indians at work and of family scenes in the villages, the exhibit included an array of their basket work. Some baskets were large and woven so tightly they could hold water, some were about the size of a thumbnail. All of them had intricate and distinctive designs, and a few even had leather thongs, feathers or beads worked into the weave.

The photographs were impressive and enhanced our appreciation of a craft these people had perfected over hundreds of years. Some of the photos were of weavers—robust women gathering the material, preparing it for use, and sitting patiently with the children of the village, passing on their art. I was pleased that these precious photos had been preserved, and wondered if any of my work would stand the test of time. Would my pictures of the AIDS Quilt be included in any retrospectives after the cure was found? Would my images of the women of America ever hang on a gallery wall after I was gone, the way Dorothea Lange's and Diane Arbus's works do?

Depressed by the thought that my work was too contemporary to endure past my own time, I talked with the class about how negatives were made in the 1880s on glass plates with bulky cameras and printed by direct contact of coated paper on the plate. All in all, my students seemed to be enjoying the experience and learning a lot as well.

When the tour and discussion were over, the class went on to lunch, but I told Connie where to meet me with the van, and walked with some apprehension toward the county jail. After signing in and subjecting myself to a search, I was allowed to wait in the visitor's area for Leah.

This time there was no lawyer present to demand that handcuffs be removed, so we sat across the table from each other, hands folded primly after the female guard's warning, "No touching." She stood back next to the door and was, I hoped, just out of earshot if we whispered.

"Are you okay?" I asked, knowing the answer.

Leah shrugged, "I'm not sleeping very well, but I guess that's normal for a newcomer. It can be pretty noisy here at night. Having any luck convincing the police to dig a little deeper?"

"Actually, I think we have a few leads. I found a threatening note that Erin and I think Huberman wrote, and the slide for Meredith's bolo tie was in her mail box at school. We're guessing someone found it and left it in her box after Meredith lost it. Huberman could have taken the tie and destroyed the mama cat with it. We still haven't put all the pieces together, but I'm staying in touch with Erin, and as soon as there's something solid, we'll take it to Gossett."

A long lock of blonde hair fell into my eyes. I need a haircut, I thought inanely as I shoved it back into place and continued, "I can't believe so much happened outside the house that morning, and I never heard any of it. I'm hoping Veronica saw or heard something that will help."

"You gotta be kidding! Huberman?" Leah shouted incredulously before lowering her voice again as the guard moved toward us. "Could that little wimp really have killed Meredith?"

"All he needed to do was swing the sledgehammer once. She wasn't a very big woman. He might have had to work hard, but he could have moved her as far as her car."

"But he lives all the way up in Westport. If he came in his own car, how did he get away with making two trips—one in Meredith's car with her body, and another to retrieve his own car— without either of us seeing or hearing him?"

"I don't know. That's what I'm hoping Veronica will help me with."

Leah reached out, almost touching my forest-green shirt, but the guard leaned forward and she dropped her hand again. "How did you know that's my favorite color? Actually, most shades of green appeal to me, but that's my first choice."

"I didn't, but I'll try to remember that." Leah's amber eyes caught my gaze, and we communicated without words for a time.

To break the spell, she asked, "How's your class going? Did they enjoy the field trip?"

"I think so. By the way, Connie sends her best."

Leah nodded. "I'm sure as hell going to need everyone's best to get myself out of this one. I still can't believe this is happening to me. I came up here to get out the vote, and look at me—I'm not even free to go to the polls myself."

I wanted to tell her it would all work out, but the best I could manage was, "Don't say it like that. You haven't done anything you need to get out of paying for."

"No, but I haven't been real smart, either," Leah said, dejectedly. "Shit, I should have known Meredith wouldn't go off in a pique like that. She was a fighter, not a pouter. Maybe I just wanted her to have done something stupid to make me angry. It made it easier to think about leaving her. Hell, when I finally called the police, I couldn't even give them her license plate number. If I had, maybe the trail wouldn't have been so cold, and I might not be the primary suspect."

"Maybe. But even Meredith, with all her schemes, had only so many enemies. If it wasn't Huberman, it was someone else. I promise you—Erin and I will find the killer." Grasping at any straw, I remembered Martin Foster, Meredith's business partner—the man Huberman had been so worried about. Hopefully, I asked, "What did you find out about that partner of hers in Sacramento when you went to see him that Friday before the ceremony?"

"Couldn't have been Foster. He was scheduled to meet with Meredith that Saturday afternoon, but his daughter fell off a playground swing on Friday. He called Meredith right away to cancel their meeting. The kid was in neurosurgery Saturday morning, and probably ten people saw him at the hospital. He told me he and his wife bugged every nurse and resident they saw for news." With a sad smile, Leah added, "It's all true, Alix. She was still in the hospital recovering the day I saw him to discuss the provisions of Meredith's will."

"Okay," I admitted, "So it couldn't have been him. It doesn't matter," I added fiercely. "If Huberman gets checked off the list, it'll be Parisi or some other man or woman Meredith was hurting with her land grabs."

For the first time since she was brought in, Leah broke into a real smile, but there was still a touch of irony in it. "You're really out there for me, aren't you?"

"Damn right I am. I won't abandon you now."

"Now?' Leah said, with a tilt of her head. "Does that mean you will after I get out of here?"

A part of me wanted to say "never," but I was too old, with too many scars, to believe that "happily ever after" was possible just because people wanted it to be. "I guess we'll have to get you free before we can figure that out. I do care for you Leah, but it's way too soon to make any promises."

"I know," Leah said softly. She stood up to go, but parted her lips slightly and ran the tip of her tongue over the soft vermilion. I felt my vulva contract and go damp. As she nodded toward the guard, I returned her smile, appreciating her private version of blowing me a goodbye kiss.

It was early evening when I arrived back home. I took care of the kitten's needs and considered trying to get some time alone with Veronica to find out what she really knew about the morning Meredith disappeared. But the uneasy tension of visiting Leah with eyes constantly watching us, coupled with the trip on the winding mountain road, had left me with a sick headache. I wasn't convinced I could outwit even Veronica Battles enough to learn anything useful.

I put together a dinner of comfort food—macaroni and cheese with diced carrots for color, and curled up in front of the fire with the kitten in my lap and a glass of wine by my side. Genie seemed thrilled to be out of her bathroom prison, so when it was time for bed I decided to leave her out after making sure the fireplace screen was secure.

She padded silently behind me as I made my way to the study. My head still throbbing, I took one look at the short, lumpy futon, and remembered Erin's words about Meredith not being in the house anymore. I collected the clothes I had moved from the cabin, shut the study door and headed for the big bedroom. I stretched out on the bed to read for a while; the sheets were fresh and the mattress luxurious compared with the futon. When I couldn't keep my eyes open any longer, I switched out the light and reached for the second pillow. Wrapping my arms around it as I had done as a child, I tried to make my fantasy lover feel true.

I was nearly asleep when I heard a persistent scraping sound from under the bed. I assumed Genie was playing with something and tried to ignore it. When I couldn't summon my dreams to return, I turned the light back on and dropped to my knees next to the bed. Gently probing for the kitten, I muttered, "Now, do I have to put you back in jail, kiddo? Aren't you going to let me sleep?"

She was batting at something near the head of the bed. After I pulled her out, my hand found a small bag. It was from a local store, the Harbor Lights Dress Boutique, and had gotten wedged between the box spring and the wall. The paper was a bit slick and had probably slipped down there long ago. Peeking into the bag, I saw a receipt and pulled it out, curious about how long the bag had been stuck there.

It was for a lady's shell top, size 36, mint green. The description sounded vaguely familiar, and when I saw that the date was just the day before Meredith's death, I went to her closet and shuffled through every hanger. Then I checked all the drawers. There were no other sleeveless green tops anywhere. Sadly, I realized that Meredith had probably bought something new to catch Leah's attention, and had purchased her own shroud instead.

Holding the little kitten, I stroked her absently, trying to call back some piece of information that was gnawing at me. Green? Green! Veronica, of course! She had described the top Meredith was wearing when she died. But wait just a minute—the only time she could have seen her wearing that shirt was that very morning. Bingo! I let out a whoop with that realization and said out loud, "Veronica, Baby, we're going to talk, whether you like it or not."

A soft mist spotted the windows of the VW as I turned onto the road running next to the Mandarin River. A Sunday morning call from Erin had broken my restless sleep. She wanted to see me as soon as possible to plan our next move on Huberman. She also said, somewhat mysteriously, that she had another piece of news. I had promised to be there within the hour.

The auto gate at the Spread was propped open to allow me through. I closed it behind me and parked near the old Victorian house. Erin was sitting across from Willow on the rockers in the garden where I had talked with her ten days ago when I was "checking out the residents." It was where I had learned more about Leah's infatuation with me and never dreamed that either one of us would truly act on it.

"Sitting out in the rain?" I called, dodging puddles as I trotted up the uneven path.

Willow waved nonchalantly. "After the past five years of drought, a warm rain like this so early in the season feels like a blessing, but if you'd rather go in..."

"No, it's fine," I said wondering if we'd remain outside if the precipitation got worse, as the sky indicated it would. Years of lugging heavy photo equipment while trudging through forests and deserts and troubled cities to get my photographs had given me a sense of my own strength, but around these women I felt like a damn sissy.

Willow's pale yellow shirt was very damp and clung to her thin shoulders. Erin had on a mauve jacket that shed the rain and made me feel a little less like a wimp in my own water repellent jacket. They stood up to greet me just as the sky opened up, sending a torrent of water down to drench us. With a laugh, Willow put her arm around my shoulders and led me toward the house. Erin followed close behind.

While Willow put on water for tea, Erin disappeared, returning with three rather thin towels. She handed one to me, then tossed the second one over Willow's head and rubbed vigorously to dry her hair. The third one she wrapped around Willow's shoulders after peeling off the saturated shirt.

Willow watched Erin go off again, then began blotting the dampness from her neck, shoulders and small but still firm breasts. "I think she's tryin' to mother me, of all things."

Softly I said, "Maybe she just cares for you."

Willow nodded, conceding the point, but added, "I s'pose, but I think it's her way of tryin' to convince herself she needs to stay here."

"And you don't want her to?"

With a sad sigh, Willow said, "I never want any of these women to leave. It's so much more dangerous out there in the world. But Erin fought hard to get her education and she has a great desire to do good things as a lawyer. I don't think she'd be happy if she turned her back on the law for good."

Erin returned with a dry zippered sweatshirt for Willow, who took it from her before Erin could wrap it around her. She thanked Erin for all her fussing, then went to fetch the tea. After we were settled on the well-used sofa and chairs in the sitting room, Erin flipped the pages of her yellow legal pad while Willow sipped her tea for a moment and I waited expectantly for the news Erin had promised.

"First," Erin said triumphantly, "I ran a trace on that white pickup truck in your photographs. It's registered to Charlie Samuels. He runs an auto repair shop on McPherson Street in Fort Bragg. I tried both his shop and home numbers this morning. No answer at the shop, but some teenage male at his house said his dad would be back tonight and the shop would be open for business at 7:30 Monday morning."

I shook my head. "I don't understand it. Who is this guy, and why would he be following Meredith?"

"No idea," Erin said. "That's why I need your help tomorrow. I want both of us to meet with Gossett tonight, and depending on how that turns out, I may be headed over the hill to Ukiah tomorrow to present our case directly to the D.A.'s office."

With exasperation, I said, "Speaking of the district attorney, shouldn't his office or the sheriff's department be doing all this investigating, not us?"

Bitterly Erin replied, "Hell, this county is practically bankrupt. That's one of the things I'm going to try to point out to them. They're wasting a lot of valuable time and money prosecuting Leah on the kind of evidence they've got. Sure, some of it implicates her, but a hell of a lot of it points nowhere at all."

After a brief silence which only heightened my feeling of helplessness, Willow set down her cup and said softly, "There's something else, Alix. Meredith didn't try to have us evicted."

I sat up straight. "You know who gave the police the phony drug tip?"

Willow shook her head. "No, I don't have a name, but some woman called here day before yesterday morning and apologized for makin' trouble for us. She was almost hysterical, sayin' she'd had nothin' but misery since she told that lie about marijuana and other drugs on the Spread. She wanted to know if we had put a curse on her."

I looked at Erin for a reaction or a question, but she was quiet while Willow continued.

"I tried to tell her we don't use our spirituality for revenge, but she just kept babblin' about how she had wanted to get back at Meredith for somethin' and was hopin' we'd drive her away from the Spread if we thought she had turned on us."

"Babbling?" I asked, trying to make sense of it all. "But you didn't recognize her voice?"

"Couldn't place it at all. Darn sure it's no one I've ever met. She talked faster than a snake's tongue can move. Ravin' about Meredith and how she was comin' on to you and it pissed her off. Now Meredith was dead, too, and that she never got anything she really wanted."

Suddenly it came to me. "Veronica Battles! It must have been her. She thought of Meredith as her personal property, and for a very short time, Meredith had invited that notion. Then when Meredith thought there was even a slim hope of reconciliation with Leah, she dropped Veronica. But Veronica didn't like taking 'no' for an answer."

Erin sat up straighter then. "But why would she take it out on the women out here?"

"I don't know," I said quickly. "Maybe she thought if Meredith was suspected of jeopardizing women on the Spread, Leah would get angry and dump her. What she couldn't know was that Leah was planning to end it with Meredith even before she came to Fort Bragg. And Meredith was embarrassed about her lapse with Veronica anyway. Besides, it wouldn't have made any difference. Meredith was through with Veronica a week before she died."

While making notes on her yellow pad, Erin mused, "How hard would Veronica have taken rejection by Meredith? Hard enough to kill her, maybe even accidentally, by taking a swing at her with the sledgehammer?"

I thought about it for a minute. "It could have happened that way. I found something last night that indicates Veronica saw Meredith the morning she died." I recounted finding the receipt from the dress shop and looking for any other article of clothing that might match the description on the sales slip. "I've been trying to catch Veronica at home and alone for a couple of days now, but her husband, Bert, seems to be sticking real close to the nest these days."

With a slap of her legal pad on the arm of the chair, Erin got up. Nodding in my direction, she said, "Looks like the rain's stopped. Are you up for a little visiting today?"

"Visiting?"

Erin nodded. "There are just too damn many loose ends in this case. First, I want to confront Huberman about his actions. Then we can both try to corner Veronica Battles. Either way, I want us to end up at the sheriff's office by tonight to lay out for him everything we've found so far."

Willow rose and stood between us. "I'm going with you."

Erin shook her head. "No, it could be dangerous." Before Willow could protest being thought of as too fragile for the job we were going to do, Erin took Willow by the shoulders and looked deep into her eyes. "I need you here knowing our plans. If there is danger, I don't want Doris involved—she has a kid to think about. And Casey, well, frankly..." Her voice trailed off, then she finished, "Let's just say, you're the only one I genuinely trust."

Somehow I knew that Willow still suspected Erin of trying to protect her, but she accepted the role of lookout graciously, if reluctantly. Erin proposed that we drive up to Westport and confront Huberman with our suspicions. Not surprisingly, she had been unable to get the police to talk to him again, even after showing them the written threat and the bolo slide. Then, after checking in by phone with Willow, we would try to see Veronica before meeting with Gossett at the sheriff's substation.

As Erin went off to call Gossett to make an appointment, I laid my hand on Willow's forearm. "She's right, you know. Besides, three people would be too many for a standoff with Huberman or Veronica."

"Probably she's right, but I don't appreciate being treated like an old lady."

"I don't think Erin sees you as an old lady at all. Unless I've completely lost my sixth sense, I'd guess she's more than a little bit in love with you."

Willow lowered her eyes. "So you've seen it, too? I thought I was seein' things, but sometimes the way she looks at me gives me the shivers."

"Any thoughts on what you're going to do about it?"

"Do?" she asked in surprise. "There's nothin' to do. She'll take that job like she's s'posed to, and she'll get over me in a hurry."

"Does she have to get over it? Aren't you even a little attracted to her, even though she is pretty young?"

"I'm almost twice her age, but that doesn't really have anything t'do with it. In some ways, Erin's pain has made her heart very old, and by living here among younger women and their children, mine's been able to grab hold of some of their wonder and zeal. But it's just not right for either of us.

"I've spent a fair amount of time before the Goddess, meditating and asking for guidance. We each have our places in this world, and for Erin and me, our places are far apart."

I wanted to believe Willow when she said age differences didn't matter, but I was still uncertain about how Leah and I could weather not only the twelve-year disparity in our ages, but the other hurdles that threatened to obstruct our relationship.

✦ ✦ ✦ ✦ ✦

Later, in the VW on our way to Huberman's home in Westport, Erin and I rehearsed our approach. Since he thought of me as an underling and a temporary employee at that, we agreed Erin would ask the questions, while I backed them up with what I'd found in Meredith's locker and mail slot.

I noticed that not only had the rain stopped, but the sun had broken through by the time we got out of the car. There was no answer at Dr. Huberman's front door, but the sound of Chopin "Études" from the backyard of the smallish white clapboard house signalled his presence. We walked around to the back and found him seated in a wooden folding chair in front of an easel, paint brush in hand. At his side, a small table held a jar of tan water. Next to that was his palette, on which he had mixed some browns and oranges, with white to lighten them. The image on the canvas was of an ancient wooden water tank, whose model stood about fifty feet away from the artist in a neighboring yard. The sun, struggling to maintain its position in the still-damp atmosphere, gave the tank an eerie quality. A large, tawny hawk perched on the water tank, eyeing the wet grass below, looking for movement that would betray some small field mouse or vole. A great time for some "painterly" landscapes, I thought, trying to recall where my cameras were lying back at the house.

Almost simultaneously, Erin and I noisily cleared our throats.

"Why, Ms. Nicholson, Alix! What brings you up this way?" He turned and looked anxiously at Erin, but didn't stand up, ask her name, inquire about her identity, or otherwise acknowledge her presence.

"Dr. Huberman," I said, sweeping my hand toward Erin, "this is Erin Reilly. She lives on the Spread on the Mandarin River. She's the attorney representing Ms. Claire on the murder charge."

Huberman's eyebrows raised slightly as he inspected Erin in her waterproof jacket, blue jeans and white running shoes. "An attorney?"

Erin stepped close to him and gave him a no-nonsense look. "Yes, Dr. Huberman. I'm investigating the murder of Meredith Coates, and since you were a colleague, I'd like to ask a few questions." Without waiting for Huberman's response, Erin continued, "Alix tells me that you weren't on very good terms with Meredith Coates."

"Well, I, that is...we didn't agree on the future course of Pacific Arts College. Nevertheless, we maintained a civil professional relationship."

"And you never threatened to 'get even with her,' either to her face, or as a promise to yourself in your office?"

Huberman shot me a sharp glance, but shrugged nonchalantly. "Merely a figure of speech, an ill-advised outburst after a rather raucous faculty meeting. Surely, you can't believe I had anything to do with her murder?"

Erin paused in her skillful questioning long enough to look into the folder she carried and pull out the note I had found. "And is this a figure of speech, too, Mr. Huberman?"

Huberman jumped to his feet, nearly spilling the water next to him as he attempted to snatch the note. "Where'd you get that...? I got rid of—" He suddenly realized he had stepped into Erin's trap and immediately shut his mouth. After a moment, he looked defiantly at her, "That doesn't prove anything. I was just trying to get her to stop the deal to buy up the land the college stands on. I wanted to scare her, not kill her."

Erin shrugged. "Suppose I believe you. Tell me what 'disappear, too' means. Who, or what, did you make disappear?"

Infuriated, I stepped in front of Erin and shouted, "It was that poor, helpless cat, wasn't it? You took her and then killed her to frighten Meredith." It was all I could do to keep my clenched fists at my side.

"Oh, what are you getting so excited about? It was just some mangy stray. But on the Wednesday before she disappeared I heard her talking about it to another faculty member. She seemed to dote on the damn thing. The next day, when I knew both of you were in class, I went out to her place and snatched it. I was just planning to frighten her a bit—to gain some leverage. But when I heard her business partner was coming out to the coast, I knew she was still hell-bent on destroying the arts program...maybe the whole school. That's when I decided to kill the cat and send her the dead animal as a threat—to scare her into dropping her scheme."

Erin was silent for a moment, considering her next question. I could barely look at this man who professed to be a lover of art, but had no regard for a living, breathing creature.

Finally, Erin continued her questioning with a cold look in

her eyes. "Again, suppose I give you the benefit of the doubt about Meredith's murder. How did your four-legged victim end up under her body in the sea cave?"

Huberman lunged toward us again, knocking back his folding chair, which collapsed in the damp grass. "What? The police never said anything about that? My God, is someone trying to frame me?"

With a satisfied smile, Erin nodded. "So the police have been here? I take it you haven't bothered to tell them about your little venture into animal control? What did you do with that poor creature's body, and when, Mr. Huberman?"

"I...I left it on the floor of her car next to the gas pedal. That was Friday night after midnight. I parked as close to her place as I could get without being seen, and carried that disgusting thing in a sack for almost a quarter of a mile." He looked from Erin to me with a nervous twitch. "I...I left a note with it. Did the sheriff find it, too?"

"Another note? And what did this one say, Mr. Huberman?" Erin looked at him as if he was a bug she wanted to squash.

"I...I don't remember exactly. I guess I said something about how did she like having something in her life strangled."

"And?"

Huberman hung his head and muttered evasively, "And I said perhaps the same thing could happen to her."

Erin nodded to me, signalling we were done with this interview. Before turning back toward the van, I stole a peek at Huberman's painting again. The colors were well-chosen, the shape of the water tank nicely muted by the subdued light, but the hawk, the one thing that gave the real water tank its purpose and majesty, was missing from Huberman's canvas. With as much contempt as I could muster, I said, "Nice technique, Roald. Too bad it lacks heart."

By the time we were heading back down the coast it was midafternoon. Erin was talking as much to herself as to me to piece it together. "If Huberman didn't kill Meredith, then the killer must have seen the cat carcass and possibly even Huberman's note, and recognized it as some kind of threat. That person must then have decided to try and point the finger at another one of Meredith's enemies."

"But what happened to the note Huberman claims he left?"

Erin spread her hands in a gesture of uncertainty. "It's hard to know. Maybe the killer overlooked it; maybe he or she left it with Meredith's body and the tide washed it out to sea."

"Are you sure now that it wasn't Huberman?"

Erin bit her lip as she answered. "Almost sure. He's a vile, self-absorbed little man, certainly. But I doubt he could translate the kind of gutlessness it took to destroy a pitiful animal into vicious action against a human being. The way he caved in to my questions without a fight doesn't jibe with the nerve needed to strike out at Meredith. Also, his walking to the house the night before explains why you didn't hear anything unusual."

Willow was right. Erin was not only very good at working for a client's freedom, she also relished the search for the truth. Her blue eyes shone as she attempted to untangle the fatal strands of events that led to Meredith's death.

"Does that mean you think the killer also walked onto the property?"

"Maybe. We know the killer took Meredith off the property in her own car; the blood the forensics team found in it proves that. Perhaps it served several of his needs. One, a way to transport the body without leaving traces in his own vehicle; two, a way for the killer to get away from the scene; and three, since you were familiar with the sound of Meredith's car starting up, it didn't break into your sleep."

Erin's eyes dropped to her legal pad as she jotted down some notes on her theory. Staring out the window, I said, shaking my head, "Damn. I still can't believe all that went on practically outside my window. I don't care if it *was* midnight when Huberman says he was there, or in the morning when Meredith disappeared. God, I must have been out cold."

When we stopped at the Spread for Erin to pick up her own car, there was a message from Gossett postponing our meeting until Monday evening. I'd have to miss part of my class to join Erin at the meeting. After letting Willow know we had survived our confrontation with Huberman, the Artiste of Westport, we drove back to my home base. I pulled into the carport with Erin close behind. She killed the engine and started to walk down the drive toward the Battles's house across the road.

I trotted after her and pulled her back a step or two. "No, wait. Veronica Battles may be flighty, she may even be a murderer, but she's no doormat. If we both confront her, she'll just get surly and we won't get anything out of her. Let me do this by myself. Same rules as we had with Willow. If I don't check back in twenty minutes, come running."

Erin started to object, but she cocked her head slightly and took note of the hard look I was trying to project. "Okay, you've got twenty minutes."

After crossing the narrow road that separated the Battles's property from Meredith's, I listened for any indication that Bert was working in the yard or around the house. But the only sounds were the chatty quail on the wooded lot next to their one-story house. I crept up to the garage door and peeked in. The roof of Veronica's blue Saab sedan was visible through the small, high windows, but Bert's black Dodge Ramcharger was not in sight. Hopeful that I'd finally get to talk to Veronica alone, I tapped lightly on the front door and waited.

When there was no answer, I tried the knob and found it locked. Stepping off the concrete pad of the entryway, I slowly made my way around toward the back of the house. I wasn't sure what I was supposed to be looking for, but in a corner of the lot nearest the wooded area next door, I found it—a substantial pile of wood chips. The rose beds and garden areas were generously blanketed with them, but there was enough in the mound to cover two or three times the same amount of ground. I picked up a handful from the heap and sniffed. They were damp from the morning's rain and seemed to be from a fragrant type of evergreen, but my scant knowledge of botany took me no closer to an identification. I stuffed some chips in the front pouch of my red sweatshirt and continued my search for Veronica.

I shaded my eyes as I peered through the glass sliding door at the back of the house, but she was not in sight. With my van key, I tapped on the glass hoping to make enough noise to summon her from wherever she might be in the house. When no one appeared, I was about to give up and take my flimsy fistful of evidence back to Erin. As a last hope, I tugged on the handle of the glass door, and because the catch was loose, it slid open a crack.

I shoved the image of Bert's hulking frame from my mind as I began my first real experience in breaking and entering. It took only a

little more jiggling to dislodge the catch, then, heaving a deep sigh, I
stepped into the kitchen. A single coffee mug and plate sat in the sink.
Perhaps Bert had gone back to the city. But if Veronica wasn't home
and her car was still in the garage, maybe she had gone back with him.
Or she may have gone off somewhere with some other friend who picked
her up. It seemed odd thinking of Veronica having anyone other than
Bert, or Meredith. Her possessiveness around Meredith had made her
seem extremely needy, not the sort who would have a broad social
circle to draw from.

A hallway leading from the kitchen was lined with four doors,
two on each side. The first on the right led to a linen closet; on the left
was a large, sunny bedroom. It was impossible to tell from their closet
if Bert and Veronica had left town. Her side of the closet was nearly
full of mostly casual clothes, plus a couple of stylish skirt suits and
three dresses. He had fewer things, but that was to be expected since
he spent most of his time in Oakland.

Further down the hall I found the bathroom, which had a
sunken whirlpool tub and a tiled shower stall. The fourth door was
open to disclose a somewhat cluttered study/work room with just one
bookshelf about two-thirds full, a modest desk with a phone, an answering machine and a small pile of what looked like bills. There was
also a spiral note pad next to the phone. With a shrug, I flipped back
the pages of the pad. There weren't many notations, but I copied down
the last three or four phone numbers to check them with Erin. After a
rather cursory look around the sitting room, I decided I had probably
wasted most of my twenty minutes and was giving Erin a heart attack
back at the house. With one last look at the desk, I spotted a large
manila envelope with what looked like the edges of photographs sticking out.

There were two 8x10 black-and-white photographs, both shot
looking into the Battles's bedroom. In one Veronica was grasping the
lapels of Meredith's shirt as she pulled it down past her elbows, revealing her firm, erect breasts. In the second picture, Meredith was
completely nude and Veronica was on her knees caressing the soft,
hairy mound between Meredith's legs. Clipped to the photos was a
business card that read RICH MEYERS, PRIVATE INVESTIGATIONS
with a San Francisco address and phone number. On the back was a
terse note. "$200,000 for the negatives." My heart was pounding. Here

was proof that Bert knew about Veronica's affair—a classic motive for murder. Did I dare take these pictures away to show them to Gossett? Throwing caution to the wind, I slipped the pictures back into their envelope, pulled up my sweatshirt and tucked the envelope in the waistband of my jeans.

Just as I reached the glass door in the kitchen, I heard the rumble of a heavy vehicle start down the drive. Pulling up the hood of my sweatshirt to conceal my identity in case Bert caught sight of me, I slipped out the door and dashed across the lawn. It was nearly dusk, but as I headed toward the wooded lot adjacent to their house, I was wishing it was later in the day. I could have used the cover of a dark night. I jumped lightly over a fallen tree at the edge of the woods and took a dive behind the stump of a massive redwood cut years ago.

Bert Battles left his car outside of the garage and was digging in his pocket for the front door key. I was fairly sure he hadn't seen me leave his property, but I decided to stay quiet until he was safely in the house and couldn't hear me stepping on twigs as I made my way back to the road. Pressing my forehead against the rough stump, I prayed to the robust goddess on the Spread that my twenty minutes weren't up and Erin wouldn't race down the driveway yelling for me.

From my vantage point I finally saw the light in the sitting room switch on, and after another minute or so, the flickering reflections of light from a television screen. Carefully, I moved away from the stump and worked my way through the dense underbrush toward the road. Brambles from the wild blackberries clawed at my hands and snagged the hood of my shirt. As I broke through the branches of another prickly shrub, my foot found the soft shoulder and I saw Erin just crossing the road from Meredith's place.

"No!" I called in the loudest whisper I could manage.

Erin turned at my voice and broke into a grin. "Damn. I'm glad to see you. I watched Bert pull up and wondered if you had gotten anything out of Veronica."

"She's not there," I said, taking Erin's arm and leading her back to the house. I described my adventure in breaking and entering and showed her the photographs with trembling hands.

"Alix, dear Goddess, this is dangerous. If the Battles find those missing, they'll be sure to know you or I had something to do with it."

"I know, Erin, but I only need them for a little while. I can make positives of the prints, then new prints from the positives. And now that I know there's a faulty latch on the Battles's back door, I can replace these the next time their house is empty."

Shaking her head, Erin cautioned, "You're getting to like this burglary stuff too much, Nicholson. Just be very careful. Those photographs won't prove that Bert Battles is a murderer, only that he or Veronica are being blackmailed by someone. But whether he's a killer or not, my guess is that Bert could be very violent."

Carrying coffee mugs, we settled in the sun room. Although the light was gone, it was more comfortable than Meredith's sitting room. Erin said, thoughtfully, "The question is, who took those photos and why? Maybe we'll know more after you find out about that truck."

"The truck?"

"Sure, the times you say you saw it parked near Highway 1, whoever was in it could have been watching Veronica just as easily as Meredith."

With a stretch and a yawn, Erin continued, "You said you copied a couple of phone numbers? Better let me see them before I fall asleep on you. It's been a long day."

I dug out the slip of paper I'd pulled from the note pad and handed it to Erin. Immediately she tapped the edge of the page with a flick of her middle finger. "You were right! Veronica was the one who planted the phony drug tip with the cops. This last one is the number of the main house at the Spread. Veronica Battles wouldn't have any other reason to call there."

With that theory confirmed and the photographs in hand, we were precisely no closer to getting Leah free than we had been yesterday. I had hoped for some kind of miracle that would give Gossett the insight to see Leah's innocence, but I knew only the facts could accomplish that goal, not the fates.

On Monday morning, I got up well before daylight to get to the photo lab before any students arrived. Since there was no way of knowing how long it would take to link the photographs to other evidence, I wanted to make copies of the prints and return the originals as soon as possible. Maybe the theft had already been discovered, but I was counting on the notion that whichever of the Battles was being blackmailed wouldn't want to review the prints very often. Of course, I could have just made photocopies on a copier, but I wanted real photographic images. I tried not to jump to the conclusion that just because Bert or Veronica was being blackmailed, one of them also had to be a killer.

It wasn't even six a.m. when I arrived at the college. I searched through my boxes of photographic paper and large-size negative film until I found the positive film I needed to transfer the prints. By laying a sheet of this film over the photograph and exposing them under the enlarger, I could transfer the image onto the positive. With a fresh sheet of photographic paper under the positive, I could make a reproduction of the print.

I was about to take the prints into the darkroom when something about them made me look twice. The surface! There was a faint "pebbly" quality to the surface that was different from most paper. Without even pulling a sheet for comparison, I knew where I had seen that texture before—the sample papers I had gotten for my classes! Besides Connie, six or seven other students had taken packets of paper when they were offered, but I thought I knew who had printed these shots. Tony O'Keefe would do anything for a buck, and I remembered that he had been brazen enough to place an ad in the local paper offering developing services before I told him he'd get kicked out of class if I saw anything but class assignments in the darkroom.

Confronting him could wait. Right now I had to get the copies made. After making and developing the positives, I slipped them into the film dryer and set the temperature on high. When they were dry enough to work with, I made the prints and washed them. Not wanting to waste time drying the prints, I slipped them into a blotter book and headed for the VW to carry out the next of my day's assignments designed to get Leah out of jail—and the real killer into one.

Promptly at 7:30, Charlie Samuels appeared outside his car repair shop. The big, two-story, wood-shingled building with wide-swinging double doors was painted tan and looked as if it had once been a barn, with a loft or a garage for school buses.

Samuels only glanced at me, but took a long, appreciative look at my old but well-maintained VW bus. "Yes, ma'am? Can I help you? Got a problem with your grand old lady there?"

With a grin, I nodded at my reliable old companion. "No, she...um...it's fine. I just had a couple of questions." As I reached for the photographs of his truck, I had a sudden inspiration about how to get the information I needed from Samuels without letting him know I was curious about Meredith's murder. Using my pen as a pointer, I indicated his truck in one of the pictures.

"Mr. Samuels, I'm a photographer. In fact, I'm teaching a couple of classes at Pacific Arts this fall. I was just snapping shots around the parking lot last month, and, almost by accident, I came up with this one. Is this your truck?"

"Yeah," he shrugged, "what's so special about it?"

"Well, see how that other car is reflected in the side window? That adds a lot of interest to a shot. I'd like to see if one of the publishers of beginning photography textbooks would be interested in publishing it. But I'd also like to get a release from you, mainly because your license plate is showing. I could burn it off the print in the enlarger, but I think this makes it look all the more authentic."

Samuels shrugged again, "I s'pose it's okay."

As I drafted a handwritten release form on a yellow legal pad, my hand paused over one blank space. Innocently, I asked, "By the way, Mr. Samuels, do you recall what day it was you parked your truck in the college lot?"

"Weren't me, lady. That truck is a loaner I keep for customers to use while their wheels are in the shop. When did ya say you was shootin' them shots?"

"About a month ago."

Samuels thought for a moment. "Early October, eh? Lemme think." He went to his cash register and lifted out some credit card slips. "Mebbe it was this guy. First, he brung in his car, a nearly new Buick with almost no water in the radiator. I loaned him the truck and checked out that car for two days, but couldn't find no leak."

It took considerable restraint not snatch the credit card carbon from Samuels to get the name, but instead I asked reasonably, "And that was the only time this man had the truck?"

"No, that's the funny thing. He come back twice more with some story about needing a truck to haul some firewood while he was renting a house down south of town. I told him to just go over to the Rent-all place, but he said he wanted an open bed to toss stuff into. He paid me pretty good, so I said 'what the hell.' Guy wants to drive that old clunker a couple of days, why not?"

I wanted to scream at this slow-moving but genial man, "The name dammit, the name." But again, I bit my lip and asked softly, "May I ask who he was?"

With a tilt of his head, Samuels showed me one of the credit card slips. The imprint read R. D. MEYERS. *Meyers? The private investigator was following Meredith, too? And what was his connection to Bert Battles?* Sliding the makeshift release toward Samuels, I said, "I guess it doesn't matter who had it. It's your truck. If you'll just sign here, I won't trouble you anymore."

Back at the college, I lectured on using long exposures and alternate light sources instead of a flash in documentary situations where a flash could be intrusive. As I spoke, I could barely wait to get Tony O'Keefe alone. After about twenty minutes of lecture, I let the class go back to work in the darkroom, but put a hand on Tony's arm to get his attention. He was a slight young man, about nineteen, with jet black hair and cornflower blue eyes framed with long, dark lashes. Those blue eyes now gazed at me with a practiced look of innocence. To avoid interruption, I escorted him into an adjacent empty class-room.

Before I could begin my questioning, he blurted out, "Honest, Ms. Nicholson, I haven't done any free-lancing since you caught me last time."

Struggling to keep my tone as neutral as possible, I said, "That was only two weeks ago, Tony. I just happened onto something a little older than that. I want to know if this is your work, or if you printed these for someone else."

Without another word, I pulled the two photographs out of the envelope and shoved them in his direction. His soft, girlish hands that reminded me so of Brian shook slightly as he reached for the prints.

He was silent for a time, then the words, in breathless fear, came spilling out of him. "I didn't take these, I swear. I would never spy on anyone like that. I didn't even know what was on the film until I developed it. I did the film and the prints for this guy who needed 'em quick. I didn't recognize no one in the shots until I was drying the 8x10's. When I saw one of those ladies was Ms. Coates, I figured I was in trouble. Then later, when she died, well...I knew I'd gotten into something real dangerous."

Waving my hand in a "slow down" gesture, I said, "Okay, Tony, okay. I want to believe you when you say you didn't take these, but I need to know who did."

Tony breathed a little easier as he continued, "Some guy stay-ing at the Sea Bird motel in town. Name's Richie, that's all I knew. He paid me $200 in cash for developing the film and all the prints."

"Just Richie?"

"Yeah, that's it," Tony shrugged, and added timidly, "ma'am."

Back at the house after class, I changed into jeans, a sweatshirt and sneakers, and trotted up the drive to see if the Battles's house was empty. Again, Veronica's Saab was still in the garage, but Bert's big car was gone. After I slipped the envelope with the pictures under my sweatshirt, I knocked on the door. Even if Veronica was home, I might be able to get back upstairs after visiting with her for a while. But there was no answer. Looking carefully around, I headed for the back door and found the faulty latch as before. I proceeded directly to the study. With a sigh of relief, I placed the envelope containing the prints back on the desk in what I hoped was the exact same spot.

As I jogged back down the drive toward Meredith's house, I couldn't help but feel that this breaking and entering stuff was getting too easy, and that sooner or later I'd be very sorry. I might have brooded longer about my increasingly checkered career as an amateur burglar, but I heard the rumble of Erin's old yellow Volvo behind me.

Waving as she got out of her car, she said, "I got back from Ukiah early. It didn't take long for the D.A. to hear me out about how wasteful of public funds pursuing this case was, but the most I could get out of her was 'I'll think about it.' But at least she listened."

Erin was as baffled as I after hearing my report. "Do you suppose Bert hired a P. I. to check up on Veronica and the guy got onto Meredith's involvement with her?" After a pause, she shook her head. "Then it wouldn't make sense for the investigator to turn around and blackmail his own client. I'll take it from here, Alix. I'll give the guy a call, but without a subpoena, he's not obliged to tell me anything, and we'd need a lot more evidence to get a subpoena of an investigator's records."

Feeling helpless and at another seemingly blank wall, I pressed Erin, "We've got all these loose ends that seem to be pointing absolutely nowhere, Erin. Is any of this helping Leah?"

"Of course it is, Alix," Erin said soothingly. "Sooner or later, and I'm betting sooner, something will crack it wide open. In the meantime, we've just got to keep digging."

After the puzzling revelations of the day I had returned home to catch my second wind. As I fixed a light dinner of tomato soup, and nibbled on the fragrant cheese bread I'd picked up at the local bakery, the thought of having to leave the house later to meet my evening class made me groan. I decided to be comfortable as long as possible, and changed into a blue-and-white sweatshirt and matching sweatpants— a comfort tip I had learned from my friend Mac in D.C.

Curling up on the couch with one of Leah's books, Alice Walker short stories, I soon found Genie snuggled in my lap as if we were set for the night. I don't know which of us was more put out—the kitten when I plucked her off my lap, or me— when I dragged myself up to prepare for another evening of novice students falling in love with mediocre negatives and wasting reams of paper trying to turn them into wondrous prints. I looked down at my outfit and thought, *Screw Huberman. I'm not climbing into uncomfortable shoes and good clothes to mess around with photographic chemistry anymore.* I traded my slippers for running shoes and stepped out the door. A damp, chilly fog had moved in so I grabbed my red hooded sweatshirt. It still smelled faintly of the wood chips Erin and I hoped to turn over to Gossett with the pictures. I tucked my hair under the hood to keep the mist off of it.

As I pulled out of the driveway onto the road, I thought I saw movement in front of the Battles's house and wondered if Veronica had finally come home. Slowing down, I realized it was Bert who was giving me a long look as I completed my turn. I hit the gas and got the hell away from his glare.

Smacking my forehead with the heel of my hand, I thought, *Real smooth, Nicholson. Just the way any old innocent neighbor would act. Not at all the guilty maneuver of a break-in artist.* I grinned at the new irony of that term—artist—that had been tossed about so lightly or uttered so pompously in recent weeks.

Only a little more than half the class turned up, and, I noted glumly, most of them were not among my favorite students. I supposed it was biased to want to spend more time with the students who showed "a good eye" for capturing images and some skill in the developing processes.

Most of the students stayed an hour or two, then left their developed prints on drying racks. Toward the end of class, I was explaining to one of the slowest students, for at least the third time, how depth of field was affected by the aperture. Somehow, I doubted that it was any clearer to him now than it had been. It was turning into a long evening.

When I returned to the darkroom to remind the rest of the class to finish up, I found that the last two or three students had slipped out through the emergency exit and left the darkroom chemistry set-ups in place for me to clean up. Cursing softly under my breath, I flipped the room lights on and the red-orange safelight off. I dumped the paper developer, because it only remains fresh a few hours after being mixed, and the stop bath, which had lost its normal yellow color and had become decidedly grey. When I tested the fix for freshness, I found it worth saving for another class. The staff had been asked to conserve supplies whenever possible.

I reached for the dark brown plastic jug in the cabinet under the developing sink and found it nearly full, but I poured what I could through a funnel into the jug. There wasn't another empty jug for fix in the darkroom so I went to get one from the supply cabinet in the classroom. I took a few extra minutes to straighten up the chairs for the next teacher's morning class and to make up another, more pointed sign about cleaning up the darkroom after every class. If I didn't hurry, I'd be late for the ten o'clock meeting with Gossett and Erin.

Returning to the darkroom, I spotted a tray of fix on the counter, and felt a faint draft from the emergency exit. It made me swear softly about students who wanted to be treated like adults, but still dodged responsibility like adolescents. And as I went around the counter that held the developing sink to close the door, I heard a slight scuffling on the other side. Before I could turn the corner to check it out, a form leaped at me over the edge of the sink counter and pulled me back by the collar of my sweatshirt, nearly choking me. My arms still free, I managed to twist around and throw the tray of photo fix at my attacker. It wasn't caustic or particularly dangerous, except to the eyes, but the action startled my assailant just long enough to allow me to pull free. I raced for the light switch and flicked it off just in time. Darkness would be to my advantage in this familiar place. In the next instant, I heaved a full jug of photo chemistry at the hulking frame closing in on me. He caught it straight in the chest, and after a surprised "Ooommph," the attacker muttered "bitch," and I recognized the voice of Bert Battles.

Though it was dark, I could see he was blocking my way to the emergency exit. I was afraid to try and escape through the alcove that served as a light lock between the darkroom and classroom. If he caught me there, his size could easily block my exit from either door.

He grunted at me, "You were snoopin' around in my house, bitch. You're gonna pay for that."

I circled around the center counter and realized I might have a chance at the emergency exit if I moved quietly enough to keep him from turning around. Holding my breath, I inched my way toward the exit until I was about two strides from the door. As a tremendous rush of adrenaline surged through me, I stood up and made a break for the door. I flung myself out just as he turned around. With my running start, I managed to elude his grab for me. With a profound thanks to the goddess, I pulled my ring of keys from my sweatpants pocket. I had slipped them in there only after unlocking the supply cabinet in the classroom. If I hadn't needed the fresh jug, I'd be trying to outrun Bert Battles while my car keys sat safely in my pack in the classroom.

I blessed her again when the VW sprang to life at the first twist of the ignition key. The coastal fog had been causing the old engine to balk at starting for weeks now. I maneuvered around the few remaining cars in the parking lot. Briefly I considered staying on the campus and trying to get help from one of the cars' owners, but the maze of classrooms and faculty offices showed more lights than there were cars. It would be hard to know where anyone else might be. Sometimes, even the library was unattended. No, I decided, the safest escape was on wheels, and the surest place for help was the local police station in town. It was closer than the county office where Erin and Gossett would be waiting.

I was almost out of the parking lot driveway when I saw Bert sprinting for his Ramcharger. There was no way the little VW engine could outrace him for long, and I cringed at the thought of him banging that heavy grille into the VW's rear engine. But if I could make it into town, or even to the bowling alley across the bridge, he'd attract plenty of attention trying to disable me.

My heart was pounding in my ears as I turned south onto the two-lane road and stomped on the gas. But Bert was driving like a wild man. He veered into the northbound lane and gave the VW a hard bump that sent me onto the shoulder of the road. I kept driving on the shoulder when I saw an oncoming car in Bert's lane. Surely that would make him back off. But that car's driver saw the massive vehicle heading straight for him, panicked, and with his brakes squealing, pulled off into the motel's lot.

Before I could get my van back onto the road, Bert swerved his car into me again. With no more ground to grip, the VW swayed madly, took out a couple of reflector posts and a speed limit sign, then tumbled off the shoulder and rolled down the embankment. She came to an abrupt stop, after rolling on her side, on the rough, broken path next to Pudding Creek Beach. Suspended in the driver's seat, I couldn't help but laugh at myself. Despite the imminent danger bearing down on me in the parking lot, I had taken the time to buckle my seat belt. I did a quick inventory of parts and decided I was all there. Bracing myself for another tumble, I unfastened the belt and crawled toward the roof of the VW, which lay cracked open like a giant yellow egg.

I pulled myself out and looked around to determine where Bert had ended up. The big Dodge was still upright, and Bert was backing it around to face the beach. When he climbed out, he left the headlights on so that they bathed a wide swath of sand in an arc of bright light.

As I caught my breath and leaned against the jagged rock of the embankment, I plotted my next move. Clearly, on foot, I could outrun Bert for a good long time. But if I headed toward town and he spotted me, he'd have the advantage of a fast, heavy-duty car that could climb curbs with barely a bounce. If I headed out toward the beach, there was no help at all unless I tried to climb the unused trestle bridge across the river. Suddenly, out of the corner of my eye, I caught a glimpse of light. It was then I remembered there was an old tunnel of an underpass running beneath the highway. Frantically, I tried to recall what was on the other side of the road, then decided it didn't matter.

As I scrambled up toward the tunnel, I discovered that it was lined with corrugated metal. A noisy exit at best, I thought. Better to try and distract Battles before breaking for freedom. Picking up a handful of rocks, I flung them at the VW. They made a sharp, clanging sound on impact. As Battles approached the wreck to look for me, I selected the largest of the remaining rocks and aimed for his head. Bull's-eye! As Battles doubled over, I blew a kiss to the memory of one of my former lovers, Debra, who had coerced me into pitching softballs for her batting practice.

Diving into the tunnel, I pounded through the tube until I reached a mobile home park on the other side. The first two houses were dark, and I was afraid it would take too long to wake anyone up. At the third house, where the lights were on, I sped up the four steps and frantically banged on the door. A wide-eyed, elderly woman peered at me through the glass. "Please, help me. You don't have to let me in. Just call the police. Someone's trying to kill me."

Without hesitation, the woman opened the door and hurried to dial 911 while I anxiously watched for Bert Battles. Within five minutes, a young officer appeared at the door.

"You the lady who called? The one driving the old bus?"

I pointed at the resident, a Mrs. Hurley, and said, "Yes, well, actually she made the call for me, but there's a man..."

"Yeah, lady, I know. We found him flat on his back on the sand, next to the van. You really socked it to him—his face was a bloody mess. Looks like his nose got broken real good."

"That man, he—"

"You can tell us all about it down at the station, but after checking out the condition of your car and his, I reckon you didn't try to run *him* off the road."

As I leaned back to ease the bruises I was finally able to feel, I said, "You might want to give Officer Gossett of the sheriff's department a call, too. He may have a few questions for Mr. Battles."

"Yes, ma'am. You just relax now."

Willow's soft grey eyes watched me wear a path on the braided rug in the sitting room of the old mansion. Her smile was indulgent, amused. I gave her a wide-eyed look of innocence.

"What? I can't just sit still. After the bruising I took in my late lamented bus, I'll be stiff as hell if I don't move around a little."

"Uhum," she nodded with a twinkle in her eye. "Just remember, Erin only took off for Ukiah about an hour and a half ago. It'll be mid-afternoon before she's back here with Leah. Why don't you 'move around' outside, get some fresh air? We're famous for it up here." Getting up herself, Willow added, "Whatever you decide, I'm not about to sit here and waste an entire Saturday watching you fret. I've got garden plots to put to bed for the season, and some to wake up to sustain us through the winter solstice and after."

That woman read me like a trail in the sand. I had struggled so hard to clear Leah that I had spent almost no time considering the possibility of that actually happening. Now, the prospect of seeing Leah again was making me a nervous wreck.

Despite Erin's best efforts, for five days the overburdened, under-funded county government had been unable to schedule a court date to secure Leah's release. Finally, she had threatened them with a lawsuit for unlawful detainment and had roused a judge to sign the release on a weekend. Now that they were headed back to the coast, the only question I really cared about was "what next?"

I started to follow Willow out the door, but she turned around and thrust a wide-brimmed straw hat at me. "Here, depending on where you walk, you might run into some cobwebs, especially down near the river bank. You'll want this."

I took the hat with a nod of thanks and parted company with
Willow outside the back door. She headed for her beloved plot of earth,
and I let my feet take me one step at a time away from the house. I did
make my way toward the river bank and followed a rough footpath
until it disappeared into the thick underbrush. Finally, without even
looking to see if I would land in poison oak or thistles or brambles, I
lowered my body to the ground and watched the slow-moving water
pass in front of me.

I had seen so much, felt so much, lost and found so much in a
scant two months that my chest felt too small for a heart which threatened to explode at any moment. My beloved bus, painted yellow and
black because it was the successor to my "bee-tle," was gone. A kind
of friend, Meredith Coates, was gone, too. I had kept her at arm's
length and never understood her until I heard the rest of her story
from Leah. Leah, a treasure I had lost all hope of finding—a woman
who would love me with a fervent, all-consuming desire, and a woman
I could return that kind of passion to.

Then there was the community of women I had met and come
to know, women who shared not only their space, but their energies,
their meager resources and their impressive talents. They included Erin,
who had taken up Leah's cause, and Connie, who had explored every
inch of me with her skillful nurse's hands to make sure I was all right
the night of the car crash when the police brought me here after I
refused to go to the hospital. Willow had brewed a pungent tea of pep-
permint and lemon grass to settle my stomach, which lurched every
time I relived the experience of the bus careening sideways off the
shoulder of the road. After Doris and Casey pulled a cot from the attic
and cleaned it up for me, Willow had sat beside it holding my hand
and humming softly until I was asleep.

I wasn't sure how long I sat on the river bank, but finally the
slanted rays of sun on the smooth river told me it was well past noon.
Standing up, I realized my prediction about getting stiff from sitting
too long had come true. To limber up, I did a slow trot back along the
river path, then made my way up to the clearing where the main house
and garden nestled. In the distance I could see Willow still raking
straw over the garden, stooping now and then to firm some clumps of
it around the bases of leafy cabbages or feathery carrot tops.

Watching Willow at her work, I was reminded that on

Monday, I would have to get back to mine. Since the assault, I had asked Connie and another advanced student to handle my class and lab. When I had called the college on Friday to discuss with Huberman some make-up hours, my call had been forwarded to Mark Sutter. He explained that Huberman had left Pacific Arts College for an extended sabbatical and was not expected back until the following fall term, if then. When I mentioned that news to Erin, she simply smiled wisely, seeming not at all surprised.

I made a detour in the route back to the house and stopped in front of the stone Goddess. The face that seemed to gaze down at me wore a neutral, dispassionate expression, but I knew some force higher than me had conspired to save me from Bert Battles. However, I wondered if the same powers hadn't also plotted my appearance on the North Coast in the first place. "Alright," I said, feeling only slightly foolish addressing a deity I had no formal knowledge of, "I'll ask you the question. What happens next?"

I wasn't sure what I expected, but the figure remained as stoic and immovable as the stone she was. Fumbling in a small wooden box set on a pole beside the figure, I found a few candles, some white, others in various colors. I selected a yellow one and lit it with a wooden match from the box. After letting some wax drip onto a flat stone in the circle at the Goddess's feet, I set the candle into the pool of wax.

Stepping back, I felt a hand slip around my arm to make a link. I turned to find Leah's brown eyes shining so brightly they were almost the color of topaz. "What...when did you get...?"

"A few minutes ago. I told Erin to fly down those curves on Highway 20."

Without another word, I had her in my arms, kissing her mouth, cupping her soft hair in my hands to press her closer to me, squeezing the breath out of both of us with our hunger. When we finally had to break contact to take in oxygen, Leah began to lead me back toward the house. "Come on. Everyone's waiting to hear what Erin found out from the sheriff. I made her promise to wait until we were there."

"Didn't she tell you everything on the way back from Ukiah?"

Leah gripped my arm tighter and said softly, "She told me most of it, but I'm still not clear on how it all fits together. My mind was really on what was waiting for me a few miles down the road."

✦ ✦ ✦ ✦ ✦

When we arrived at the main house, Willow was casting her usual spells, pouring a fragrant herb tea that seemed to have a lot of lavender in it. Connie and Doris had brought in a pair of folding lawn chairs, while Casey and Erin shared a small love seat. The long sofa had been left vacant. I took Willow's hand and made her join Leah and me on it.

Taking her cue as the matriarch, as well as their spiritual guide, Willow raised her cup as a salute to Leah. "We thank the Goddess for the return of our sister, Leah Claire, from her imprisonment. And we thank the Goddess, also, for protecting our new sister, Alix."

The gathering of women murmured, repeating the toast, then sipped in silence for a long moment. When Erin put down her cup, she began, "Actually, Sheriff Gossett was pretty embarrassed about the whole thing." Perhaps realizing that her beginning might have sounded like an apology for the man, she quickly added, "As well he should be. I got out of him a confession that, even though he had a warrant for Leah's arrest the day he came to Meredith's house, he wasn't going to serve it just then. He only wanted to question Leah again. But get this, he decided to take her in after seeing her with Alix."

"What?" I was almost out of my seat, but Leah held fast.

"Take it easy, Alix," Erin continued. "He just thought he had more evidence for a motive, plus, as I explained to you before, you being from out of state made Leah a flight risk in his eyes."

Muttering, "God, cop reasoning strikes again," I took a deep breath and tried to let Erin get on with her report.

Standing up, Erin began to present her case as if she were facing a jury, a very friendly jury, to be sure. "Sheriff Gossett will be sending a statement to the newspapers that he has a full explanation in Meredith Coates's murder and that should completely clear Leah's name."

"Explanation?" I asked, "Don't you mean Bert's confession?"

"No, Alix. Bert didn't kill Meredith. He has an ironclad alibi for the morning she died."

"What do you mean?"

Lowering her eyes, Erin shook her head. "You're going to find this hard to believe, but it was Veronica. Apparently she had been lurking outside the house early Saturday morning, waiting to catch Meredith. She must have pleaded with her for money to pay this black-mailing investigator. They got into an argument and Veronica pushed Meredith, who fell and hit her head on the sledgehammer." After paus-ing to let us take in the scene, Erin continued, "That's one of the rea-sons she scattered so much sawdust and wood chips in the area. It took a lot of dragging for Veronica to get Meredith's body into her car, and she figured she'd better cover her tracks with the sawdust."

I couldn't believe what I was hearing when Willow broke in. Sadly, she shook her head. "One woman doing violence to another. How pitiful. Are they sure, Erin? Did Veronica confess?"

Erin nodded, "They're sure. They found a partial palm print of Veronica's on the floor mat next to the Explorer's gas pedal. It's not a place the police would normally dust for prints, but after I told Gossett where Huberman had left the cat's body, they decided to check it out. She must have leaned one hand there to move the cat so she could drive Meredith's car to the bluff above the harbor."

I pressed Erin again with Willow's other question. "But there's been no confession from Veronica, has there?"

In answer, Erin said, simply, "Alix, Bert Battles is no rose fancier."

"But I saw him spend days raking and cutting...." I stopped, somehow knowing what Erin was going to tell us next.

"He fussed with some old beds, yes, but mainly he was trying to cover up a fresh bed he had dug a few days ago after he killed Veronica and dumped her body there."

I pressed both of my hands to my head, trying to absorb it all. I started to ask another question, then just said, "Erin, go on. I'm having trouble making sense of all this."

A cynical smile played on Erin's lips. She looked like she was ready to face the big city bad guys again soon. "As well you might. First, there's the blackmailer, Rich Meyers. He was hired by Bert's opposition in the union election to find out if Bert was skimming money from the union treasury. Meyers couldn't read a balance sheet to save his life, so he tried to smear Bert with the pictures he took. His em-ployer fired him, refusing to stoop to a smear campaign. So what does Richie do? He decides to make his fee some other way. He sends copies of the prints to Veronica.

"Despite what Veronica had told Meredith about Bert's liberal attitudes, he wasn't so open about their marriage. Veronica was desperate to get those pictures back."

Erin took one of the straight-back chairs, turned it and straddled the seat, leaning on the back with her arms. "Later, after the argument that ended up with Meredith getting killed, I think she got it into her head that she was being cursed because of her phony tip about drugs on the Spread."

Willow nodded, "That's almost exactly what she said to me. Somehow, she thought her action against us had brought her bad luck."

Erin shrugged, a smile playing on her lips. "Well, you have to admit, things got pretty bad for her right after that. First the blackmail, the fight with Meredith, then Meredith ending up dead." With a wink, she added, "You sure you didn't know who the tipster was?"

Willow's eyes turned a cool, flat grey as she chided Erin, "You know our beliefs won't allow us to cause harm to any woman, Erin. I'm surprised you'd even suggest that in jest."

Properly chastened by Willow's words, Erin continued in a serious tone. "Anyway, Bert overheard her call to Willow and saw how upset she was. In his confession to Gossett he admitted comforting Veronica to find out what was going on. Apparently she was so hysterical by then, she couldn't see through his act and told him everything—the affair, the blackmail, the murder and her cover-up. Of course the bastard knew immediately he'd have to get rid of her to avoid an investigation of his private life. Turns out, he was indeed skimming money from the union local, and since he had already lost his bid for a regional job, he sure didn't want to lose the job he had, or worse, wind up in prison for embezzlement."

Casey slammed her fist into the wood paneled wall without even flinching as she cursed, "God damn them all! He consoles a confused woman in pain, his own wife for Christ's sake, and then he kills her to save his own skin."

After a moment's silence to honor and share Casey's justified indignation, I couldn't wait any longer for Erin to make her final point. "And that's why Bert came after me. He probably figured I knew more than I actually did."

"Essentially. He didn't know what you were onto, but he recognized your sweatshirt when you drove by him Monday night as the same one he'd seen running away from his house the night before. He said, for all he knew, you were another private dick trying to blow his scam." We all laughed at Erin's slang, but there was little humor in our hearts.

Willow tried again to change the facts. "But, Erin, if Veronica is dead, how can the police be so sure she did the killing?"

"They're basing it on her palm print mostly, plus a few strands of hair found next to Meredith's body matched Veronica's. Also, although Alix apparently slept through Veronica's argument with Meredith, another neighbor did hear them exchange words while she was gardening. She didn't think anything of it, because, like most of us, she didn't believe Veronica was capable of murder. Gossett tracked her down based on her earlier statement, and got her to be more specific about the details of what she heard. And, it makes sense that Veronica would abandon the car near the harbor and point the finger at Pete Parisi. She knew Pete had threatened Meredith."

We all leaned back to take a deep breath and assimilate the dramatic torrent of information Erin had spewed out. I thought about the errant palm print that led to all the other revelations and realized that the mama cat had contributed her part to finding the truth as well. The energy of life forms seemed to last well beyond their time as living beings on the planet. I looked at Willow and found her regarding me with the same detached smile I had seen on the stone Goddess. We nodded at each other in understanding.

The remaining loose ends were few, but my bewildered brain needed every *i* dotted and every *t* crossed. "But Erin, I'm still wondering about that tree that was felled across Meredith's driveway."

"We'll probably never know how that happened on that score," Erin said. "Maybe it was Veronica venting her rage, or Parisi, as you suspected all along, or perhaps it was Huberman. Who knows?"

The sun was very low in the sky now and our silence was deep and sad. After all her greed, Meredith had died for the simplest of reasons. She had died because she was lonely and had chosen to seek solace with the wrong woman. Our sorrow even extended to Veronica, as much a victim of male violence as anyone, before and up to her death.

After a very long time, Leah stood up. "I need to take a walk."

Taking her hand, I rose and said, "I'll come with you."

"No," she said softly, "I have to go alone. I was wrong the last time I was here. I hadn't finished saying good-bye to Meredith. I need to do that." With a gentle squeeze of my fingers before she released them, she added, "But I'll be back soon."

At the door, Willow gave her a small oil lamp with a glass chimney. "Just in case you don't make it back before dark."

In Leah's absence I helped the women of the Spread prepare a meal of winter squash with apples, steamed cabbage and a wonderful, dense whole grain bread. When she returned we all shared the meal, conversing sporadically in hushed tones. Each of us seemed lost in our own thoughts, each groping for something to heal the hurt of two sudden, needless deaths.

Leah and I returned to the house soon after the meal was over, glad to be alone; glad to be together. It had been an incredibly long day.

Since our fiery reunion in front of the Goddess, we had clung to each other for comfort, but had not rekindled the passion. Now, moving around the spacious bedroom, we were awkward, almost shy with each other. For an instant I considered leaving Leah to the bed in the main house and returning to my cabin, but as if she were reading my mind, Leah slipped her arms around my waist from behind.

"I want you to hold me tonight, Alix. So much has happened to me, to us, in such a short time. I can't offer more than just my closeness right now."

Turning in the circle of her arms, I pulled her into my body and rested my head on the dark waves of her hair. "That's enough for tonight, Leah, my love. We have time to figure out the rest."

Epilogue

The morning color through the skylight was a leaden grey. A wild storm whipped the slender, young redwood trees and rattled branches of the older ones outside the cabin window. It was New Year's Eve and 1992 was roaring out with much sound and fury, but it couldn't compare to the storm roiling in my own head. The cabin seemed foreign to me since I had continued living in the main house with Leah after her release in November. It took only a few days of quiet dinners and a slow return to the routine of class work for me, and settling Meredith's business dealings for Leah, to remind us of the spark that had brought us together so explosively. Our lovemaking was still ardent and our questions about the future still unanswered.

There were long walks alone, with Leah, and even some with Willow, whose precious calm and wisdom led me to understand the "coincidences" which had brought me to this special place and to Leah.

And now it was time to go home. My classes had their grades, the college had a documentary exhibit hanging in a local gallery, ensuring increased publicity for the arts curriculum, and I had an empty house waiting for me in Dubuque. Carefully I packed my cameras and equipment with extra padding to help them survive being lugged through an airport and sent through the luggage check on a crowded flight from San Francisco International. I had reluctantly agreed to send one of the camera bags through luggage check so I could carry Genie inside the cabin. I had decided that ours was one relationship that would continue back in Dubuque. But tomorrow I would step on that plane and out of Leah's life, at least for a while.

I put off packing my clothes and other essentials up at the main house until later. Cleaning up the tiny kitchen area, I had a sudden idea and headed back to the main house to share it with Leah. "Let's have that special dinner we talked about down in the cabin to-night," I announced, decisively.

"Down in the cabin? Why? This place is so much more—" Leah stopped, having caught the suggestive glint in my eye.

"Yes, you're right. I want to do it there because that's where you first seduced me, young woman."

"Here we go again," she moaned. "Young woman, young lady, kiddo. Are we ever going to get past the damned fact that I'm a precocious youngster and you're a limber baby boomer?"

With a playful bump of my hip against hers, I headed off to the grocery store to find something truly special for our final dinner. "We'll see. Seven o'clock. My place."

After a dinner of scallops sautéd in garlic and butter, a wild rice pilaf, brussels sprouts with sesame seeds, and the ubiquitous California sourdough bread, we settled in front of the wood stove to savor our dessert. It was a lusciously nutty chocolate cake Connie and Doris had brought us for a solstice celebration here. It had been far too rich to eat all at once so I had frozen half for a special occasion. Between sips of coffee and brandy, and nibbles of the cake, Leah and I gazed at each other, each with some version of a silly grin, wondering who would start first.

As the senior member of our relationship, I finally took the lead. "What are you thinking, love?"

"I'm thinking, I don't want this night to end. Do you really have to go tomorrow?"

"I do. One of the high schools has a six-week vacancy starting on January 10th, and I need to start looking for a new car."

Putting down her brandy, Leah took mine out of my hands and pulled me into her arms. "In a way I'm glad Bert Battles zapped that old bus of yours. I'll rest much easier thinking of you and Genie flying out of San Francisco with that insurance check in your briefcase than I would worrying about you in that tin can, trying to navigate the Sierras during one of these storms. There are so many closed roads and dangerous passes in this kind of weather."

I leaned away from her a little with mock indignation. "I beg your pardon! That 'tin can' may have saved my life. If it hadn't split open so nicely, Bert might have been able to finish me off before I got free of the bus."

A heavy stillness lay between us as we each went through our "what ifs." What if Bert hadn't been so clumsy and Leah was still in jail? What if the VW had rolled one more time and pinned me to the inside of the car? What if we had figured it out a couple of days earlier, would Veronica still be alive? And my own worst what if, that still gave me nightmares—what if I had gotten up at my usual hour of the morning? Could I have prevented Meredith's murder?

Softly, as if from a distance, Leah said, "When am I going to see you again?"

For a moment I tried to make light of it. "I don't know. You got any offers to raise money for some worthy cause in Dubuque?"

Biting her lip, Leah shook her head. "San Diego, Portland, Oregon, even New York City, damn it, but nothing closer than Denver or possibly, Pueblo."

"Colorado? You'd go there, even with some groups starting a boycott drive over Proposition 2?"

"Prop 2 is why I might go there. A bunch of new organizations are trying to get off the ground—with tactics that range from civil disobedience to mounting another ballot campaign, from outing every public figure in the entire state, to just plain educating people about real lesbians and gays."

"And you want to do this?"

"Something tells me I've *got* to do this, maybe for Meredith, who died because she slept with the wrong woman. And maybe for us, so we'll be at least a thousand miles closer. I don't know. I don't have to decide right away. I've rented the house beginning the first of next week, and I'm moving back to the Spread for a month or so to try and sort things out."

This time I twisted all the way out of Leah's arms so I faced her and asked her seriously, "You've made all these decisions without even telling me about them? I don't mean asking my permission or anything, you have every right to do that. But couldn't you at least have let me in on it?"

Her lower lip slipped between her teeth again, and she looked very young and about to cry. "I thought if I didn't tell you about what was going to happen after you left, your leaving wouldn't be a reality. It doesn't make any sense, I know, and I was smart enough to know I needed to make some decisions. But I couldn't talk to you about any of it because it meant you really were going away."

I took her in my arms and let her cry quietly for a few minutes, then turned her face to mine and said in a voice so husky I barely recognized it as my own, "If you want me, I will find a way to get to Denver or San Francisco or even back here to the Spread, as soon as I possibly can. Or if I can't, I will make you want to come to me in Dubuque every chance you get. In the meantime, I'm not gone yet, and I want you very much right now."

I devoured her mouth with my lips, diving deep with my tongue to take in as much of this woman as I could before we had to say goodbye. It might have been my imagination, but as we made love, it seemed we both shed tears of joy that mingled on our cheeks and blessed us with the promise that we were not going to lose at love this time.

About The Author

Sharon and her life partner continue to live and work on the North Coast of California, and within the past year have joined Women of Mendocino Bay (WOMB) to help produce a bimonthly newsletter, *WOMB with a View*.

If You Liked This Book...

Authors seldom get to hear what readers like about their work. If you enjoyed reading this novel, why not let the author know? Simply write the author:

Sharon Gilligan
c/o Rising Tide Press
5 Kivy Street
Huntington Station, NY 11746

MORE EXCITING FICTION FROM
RISING TIDE PRESS

RETURN TO ISIS
Jean Stewart
The year is 2093. In this fantasy zone where sword and superstition meet sci-fi adventure, two women make a daring escape to freedom. Whit, a bold warrior from an Amazon nation, rescues Amelia from a dismal world where females are either breeders or drones. Together, they journey over grueling terrain, to the shining world of Artemis, and in their struggle to survive, find themselves unexpectedly drawn to each other. But it is in the safety of Artemis, Whit's home colony, that danger truly lurks. And it is in the ruins of Isis that the secret of how it was mysteriously destroyed waits to be uncovered. Here's adventure, mystery and romance all rolled into one.
Nominated for a 1993 Lambda Literary Award
ISBN 0-9628938-6-2; 192 Pages; $9.99

ISIS RISING
Jean Stewart
The eagerly awaited sequel to the immensely popular Return to Isis is here at last! In this stirring romantic fantasy, Jean Stewart continues the adventures of Whit (every woman's heart-throb), her beloved Kali, and a cast of colorful characters, as they rebuild Isis from the ashes. But all does not go smoothly in this brave new world, and Whit, with the help of her friends, must battle the forces that threaten. A rousing futuristic adventure and an endearing love story all rolled into one. Destined to capture your heart. Look for the sequel.
ISBN 0-9628938-8-9; 192 Pages; $9.95

WARRIORS OF ISIS
Jean Stewart
Fans of **Return to Isis** and **Isis Rising** will relish this third book in the series. Whit, Kali, Lilith and company return in another lusty tale of high adventure and passionate romance among the Freeland Warriors. The evil sorceress, Arinna Sojourner, has evaded capture and now threatens the very survival of the new colony of Isis. As Whit and Kali prepare to do battle with a seemingly unbeatable foe, Danu makes her own plans to avenge a beloved friend's death at Arinna's hands. Eventually, high in the Cascade Mountains, they will face Arinna's terrifying magical powers.

Once again, Stewart weaves a rich tapestry of an all-women's society in the twenty-first century, bursting with life— lovers, villains, heroines, and a peril so great it forges a bond between all the diverse women of this unforgettable place called Isis. ISBN 1-883061-03-2; 256 Pages; $10.99

FACES OF LOVE
Sharon Gilligan

A wise and sensitive novel which takes us into the lives of Maggie, Karen, Cory, and their community of friends. Maggie Halloran, a prominent women's rights advocate, and Karen Weston, a brilliant attorney, have been together for 10 years in a relationship which is full of love, but is also often stormy. When Maggie's heart is captured by the young and beautiful Cory, she must take stock of her life and make some decisions.

Set against the backdrop of Madison, Wisconsin, and its dynamic women's community, the characters in this engaging novel are bright, involved, '90s women dealing with universal issues of love, commitment and friendship. A wonderful read! ISBN 0-9628938-4-6; 192 Pages; $8.95

LOVE SPELL
Karen Williams

A deliciously erotic and humorous love story with a magical twist. When Kate Gallagher, a reluctantly single veterinarian, meets the mysterious and alluring Allegra one enchanted evening, it is instant fireworks. But as Kate gradually discovers, they live in two very different worlds, and Allegra's life is shrouded in mystery which Kate longs to penetrate. A masterful blend of fantasy and reality, this whimsical story will delight your imagination and warm your heart. Here is a writer of style as well as substance.

ISBN 0-9628938-2-X; 192 Pages; $9.95

ROMANCING THE DREAM
Heidi Johanna

This imaginative tale begins when Jacqui St. John leaves northern California looking for a new home, and cruises into the seemingly ordinary town of Kulshan, on the Oregon coast. Seeing the lilac bushes in bloom along the roadside, she suddenly remembers the recurring dream that has been tantalizing her for months—a dream of a house full of women, radiating warmth and welcome, and of one special woman, dressed in silk and leather....

But why has Jacqui, like so many other women, been drawn to this place? The answer is simple but wonderful—the women plan to take over the town and make a lesbian haven. A captivating and erotic love story with an unusual plot. A novel that will charm you with its gentle humor and fine writing.
ISBN 0-9628938-0-3;176 Pages; $8.95

YOU LIGHT THE FIRE
Kristen Garrett
Here's a grown-up *Rubyfruit Jungle*—sexy, spicy, and sidesplittingly funny. Garrett, a fresh new voice in lesbian fiction, has created two memorable characters in Mindy Brinson and Cheerio Monroe. Can a gorgeous, sexy, high school math teacher and a raunchy, commitment-shy ex-singer, make it last in mainstream USA? With a little help from their friends, they can. This humorous, erotic and unpredictable love story will keep you laughing, and marveling at the variety of lesbian love.

ISBN 0-9628938-5-4; 176 Pages; $9.95

DANGER IN HIGH PLACES
An Alix Nicholson Mystery
Sharon Gilligan
Free-lance photographer Alix Nicholson was expecting some great photos of the AIDS Quilt—what she got was a corpse with a story to tell! Set against the backdrop of Washington, DC, the bestselling author of *Faces of Love* delivers a riveting mystery. When Alix accidentally stumbles on a deadly scheme surrounding AIDS funding, she is catapulted into the seamy underbelly of Washington politics. With the help of Mac, lesbian congressional aide, Alix gradually untangles the plot, has a romantic interlude, and learns of the dangers in high places.

ISBN 0-9628938-7-0; 176 Pages; $9.95

WE HAVE TO TALK: A Guide To Bouncing Back From a Breakup
Jacki Moss
Being left by your lover is devastating. Suddenly, your world has been turned into something almost unrecognizable and barely manageable. That's the bad news. The good news is that you are not the first person to be dumped, and most of those who unexpectedly find themselves in the same predicament live to love and be loved again. It's not easy. And it's not fun. But this upbeat guide with a sense of humor shows you how to survive, and eventually, even thrive.

WE HAVE TO TALK is the first interactive guide designed specifically for lesbians, to help you rebuild your life. You will recognize many of your own thoughts, feelings and fears, and find new ways of dealing with the small things in a breakup, that left unchecked, develop into big things. You will even find reasons to laugh again.
ISBN 1-883061-04-0; 160 pages; $9.99

CORNERS OF THE HEART
Leslie Grey

This captivating novel of love and suspense introduces two unforgettable characters whose diverse paths have finally led them to each other. It is Spring, season of promise, when beautiful, French-born Chris Benet wanders into Katya Michaels' life. But their budding love is shadowed by a baffling mystery which they must solve. You will read with bated breath as they work together to outwit the menace that threatens Deer Falls; your heart will pound as the story races to its heart-stopping climax. Vivid, sensitive writing and an intriguing plot are the hallmarks of this exciting new writer.

ISBN 0-9628938-3-8;   224 pages; $9.95

SHADOWS AFTER DARK
Ouida Crozier

Wings of death are spreading over the world of Kornagy and Kyril's mission on Earth is to find the cause. Here, she meets the beautiful but lonely Kathryn, who has been yearning for a deep and enduring love with just such a woman as Kyril. But to her horror, Kathryn learns that her darkly exotic new lover has been sent to Earth with a purpose—to save her own dying vampire world. A tender and richly poetic novel.

ISBN 1-883061-50-4; 224 Pages; $9.95

DEADLY RENDEZVOUS: A Toni Underwood Mystery
Diane Davidson

Lieutenant Toni Underwood is the classic soft-hearted cop with the hard-boiled attitude, and she is baffled and horrified by her newest case—a string of brutal murders, in the middle of the desert, bodies dumped on Interstate I-10. As Toni and her partner Sally search for clues, they unravel a sinister network of corruption, drugs and murder.

Set in picturesque Palm Springs, California, this chilling, fast-paced mystery takes many unexpected twists and turns and finally reveals the dark side of the human mind, as well as the enduring love between two women. A suspenseful, explosive, action-packed whodunit.

ISBN 1-883061-02-4; 224 pages; $9.99

HEARTSTONE AND SABER
Jacqui Singleton

You can almost hear the sabers clash in this rousing tale of good and evil and passionate love, of warrior queens, white witches and sorcerers.

After the devastating raid on her peaceful little village, Elayna and her brother are captured and nearly sold into slavery. Saved from this terrible fate by the imperious warrior queen, Cydell Ra Sadiin, Elayna is brought to the palace to serve her. The two are immediate foes.

But these two powerful women are destined to join forces. And so, when rumblings of war reach the palace, Cydell, ruler of Mauldar, and Elayna, the Fair Witch of Avoreed, journey to Windsom Keep to combat the dark menace which threatens Cydell's empire and Elayna's very life. But along the way they must first conquer the wild magik of their passionate dreams, learn the secrets of the heartstone, and accept the deep and rapturous love that will transcend the powers of evil.

ISBN 1-883061-00-8; 224 Pages; $10.99

EDGE OF PASSION
Shelley Smith

The author of *Horizon of the Heart* presents another absorbing and sexy novel! From the moment Angela saw Micki sitting at the end of the smoky bar, she was consumed with desire for this cool and sophisticated woman, and determined to have her...at any cost. Set against the backdrop of colorful Provincetown and Boston, this sizzling novel will draw you into the all-consuming love affair between an older and a younger woman. A gripping love story, which is both fierce and tender. It will keep you breathless until the last page.
ISBN 0-9628938-1-1; 192 Pages; $8.95

How To Order:

Rising Tide Press books are available from you local women's bookstore or directly from Rising Tide Press. Send check, money order, or Visa/MC account number, with expiration date and signature to: Rising Tide Press, 5 Kivy St., Huntington Sta., New York 11746. Credit card orders must be over $25. Remember to include shipping and handling charges: $4.95 for the first book plus $1.00 for each additional book. Credit Card Orders Call our Toll Free # 1-800-648-5333. For UPS delivery, provide street address.

Our Publishing Philosophy

Rising Tide Press is a lesbian-owned and operated publishing company committed to publishing books by, for, and about lesbians and their lives. We are not only committed to readers, but also to lesbian writers who need nurturing and support, whether or not their manuscripts are accepted for publication. Through quality writing, the press aims to entertain, educate, and empower readers, whether they are women-loving-women or heterosexual. It is our intention to promote lesbian culture, community, and civil rights, nationwide, through the printed word.

In addition, RTP will seek to provide readers with images of lesbians aspiring to be more than their prescribed roles dictate. The novels selected for publication will aim to portray women from all walks of life, (regardless of class, ethnicity, religion or race), women who are strong, not just victims, women who can and do aspire to be more, and not just settle, women who will fight injustice with courage. Hopefully, our novels will provide new ideas for creating change in a heterosexist and homophobic society. Finally, we hope our books will encourage lesbians to respect and love themselves more, and at the same time, convey this love and respect of self to the society at large. It is our belief that this philosophy can best be actualized through fine writing that entertains, as well as educates the reader. Books, even lesbian books, can be fun, as well as liberating.